Madge moved close, rested her warm hand on Judd's forearm.

The touch seared his nerves, stung his thoughts and made him waver. But God's justice took too long. His mother shouldn't have to wait.

"Judd. I like that name. Suits you so much better than Justin."

He covered her hand with his. "I like it better, too." Especially the way she said it.

"Judd, I don't want to see you hurt by taking on the role of avenger."

Caught in her steady gaze, he couldn't argue.

But he couldn't agree either.

"I'll not do anything wrong."

She lowered her eyes, leaving him floundering for determination about his course of action.

"I pray you will learn God's way is best."

He squeezed her fingers. "I appreciate that."

Neither of them moved. She kept her head down. He let himself explore the feel of her hand beneath his—strong from hard work and yet soft. Just like Madge herself.

Books by Linda Ford

Love Inspired Historical

The Road to Love
The Journey Home
The Path to Her Heart
Dakota Child
The Cowboy's Baby
Dakota Cowboy
Christmas Under Western Skies
  "A Cowboy's Christmas"
Dakota Father
Prairie Cowboy
Klondike Medicine Woman
*The Cowboy Tutor

*Three Brides for Three Cowboys

LINDA FORD

shares her life with her rancher husband, a grown son, a live-in client she provides care for and a yappy parrot. She and her husband raised a family of fourteen children, ten adopted, providing her with plenty of opportunity to experience God's love and faithfulness. They've had their share of adventures, as well. Taking twelve kids in a motor home on a three-thousand-mile road trip would be high on the list. They live in Alberta, Canada, close enough to the Rockies to admire them every day. She enjoys writing stories that reveal God's wondrous love through the lives of her characters.

Linda enjoys hearing from readers. Contact her at linda@lindaford.org or check out her website, www.lindaford.org, where you can also catch her blog, which often carries glimpses of both her writing activities and family life.

The Cowboy Tutor

LINDA FORD

Love Inspired

Recycling programs for this product may not exist in your area.

™ LOVE INSPIRED BOOKS

ISBN-13: 978-0-373-82899-9

THE COWBOY TUTOR

www.LoveInspiredBooks.com

Printed in U.S.A.

Dear Reader,

Welcome to Love Inspired!

2012 is a very special year for us. It marks the fifteenth anniversary of Love Inspired Books. Hard to believe that fifteen years ago, we first began publishing our warm and wonderful inspirational romances.

Back in 1997, we offered readers three books a month. Since then we've expanded quite a bit! In addition to the heartwarming contemporary romances of Love Inspired, we have the exciting romantic suspenses of Love Inspired Suspense, and the adventurous historical romances of Love Inspired Historical. Whatever your reading preference, we've got fourteen books a month for you to choose from now!

Throughout the year we'll be celebrating in several different ways. Look for books by bestselling authors who've been writing for us since the beginning, stories by brand-new authors you won't want to miss, special miniseries in all three lines, reissues of top authors, and much, much more.

This is our way of thanking you for reading Love Inspired books. We know our uplifting stories of hope, faith and love touch your hearts as much as they touch ours.

Join us in celebrating fifteen amazing years of inspirational romance!

Blessings,

Melissa Endlich and Tina James

Senior Editors of Love Inspired Books

This book is in special memory of my mother who faced many challenges, including the Great Depression, tuberculosis and being mother to a blended family. As I read her journals and the articles she wrote, I see a woman who was hurt time and again by events and by the people she loved, and yet she determined to show nothing but kindness. Seeing her life through her eyes has given me a deep appreciation for her spirit. May her children arise and call her blessed.

* * *

What doth the Lord require of thee, but to do justly, and to love mercy, and to walk humbly with thy God?
—*Micah* 6:8

Chapter One

Golden Prairie, Alberta, Canada
Summer, 1932

Madge Morgan groaned as steam billowed from the hood of the old clunker that served as car, truck and general chore vehicle. "Why couldn't you save your cantankerous behavior for two more blocks?" So close to her destination, yet so far. And she was late. Mrs. Crebs, her best and most demanding customer, had already warned Madge she wouldn't pay to have her laundry done unless it was delivered spotless and on time.

Madge glanced about. She could either trudge back to the center of town and the public pump for water for the radiator and get to the Crebses' late, or trundle down the street with the bundle of laundry. And still be late.

Her heavy sigh lifted her unruly bangs and provided a welcome breeze to her brow.

Better late than never. She only hoped Mrs. Crebs would agree. At least she couldn't complain about the condition of her clothing and household articles. They were crisp and spotless.

She grabbed the bundle, staggering under the weight of six sets of sheets, all nicely pressed and folded, and an amazing collection of table linens, trousers and starched shirts, all done exactly as Mrs. Crebs desired. She draped the girls' fresh dresses over her arm and plowed toward the imposing Crebs house. The stack blocked her view, but the path was straight and level right up to the front steps. Of course, she would dutifully take her armload around to the back door.

The wind pushed her dress about her legs and fought for ownership of the pile of laundry. A pair of sheets slithered sideways. Madge struggled to keep everything together. She should have tied the bundle with twine, but she hadn't expected to trundle it down the street. She hurried on her way.

And hit a wall, staggered back and lost control of her load. "No!" Her wail was far from ladylike, but she was past caring as the laundry landed in the dirt, little clouds of dust greeting its arrival.

"No. No." She swallowed back the scream tearing

at her throat. No sense in announcing her problems to the neighborhood.

She saved her fury and frustration for the source of her problem—the wall shuddering her to a halt—a living, breathing wall that grunted at her impact. "Look what you've done."

Black eyes snapped. She was certain he saw more than an ordinary man, and she almost quivered. Almost. She knew she'd never forget their intensity…nor the surprise in his voice giving it such deep tones.

"Mc? You personally own this sidewalk or something?" He picked up his battered cowboy hat and slapped it against his leg before cramming it on his head, restricting his dark, overlong hair to a thick fringe around the brim. He had a square forehead and a firm mouth.

She suddenly remembered his question. "I own my share. What are you doing in the middle of the way?"

"Standing here. Minding my own business. Is that a criminal offense? First I heard of it."

"Not criminal. Just…dumb." The accident wasn't his fault, and this whole conversation bordered on the absurd. "These things are as dirty as mud." Mrs. Crebs was going to have a kitten. Probably a whole batch of them, squalling and demanding attention. Nothing to do but pick up the items and try to explain what happened. She reached for the scattered articles, now tossed into disarray by the relentless wind.

Seems the man had a similar notion and bent at exactly the same moment. They cracked heads.

"Ow." She straightened and rubbed her brow.

"Ouch." He grabbed after his hat, getting away in the incessant breeze.

The wind increased, picked up gritty dirt and pelted them. They turned their backs into the attack and waited for it to pass.

She scooped up flapping laundry. The starched-and-ironed tablecloth was no longer gleaming white. Mrs. Crebs would be offended, especially when she heard the whole thing had been witnessed in amusement by a couple of men on the sidewalk and several ladies peeking from their windows.

The man responsible for her predicament reached for a starched and now crumpled shirt. She snatched it from him.

"Only trying to help," he murmured, sounding faintly amused.

"You've already done enough." How was she going to explain this?

Despite her protests, he helped gather up garments and piled them in her arms. Fabric draped and flapped over her shoulders. She hesitated, annoyance and worry warring with good manners.

"You're welcome," the man said, grinning widely.

It wasn't his fault. Yet whom else could she blame?

The foolishness of trying to place responsibility for this whole situation on anyone or anything was as silly as trying to attribute the drought, the depressed prices and life in general to someone. Her life, her future, was in God's hands. Not man's. Amusement smoothed her annoyance and relaxed her eyes.

He must have seen the change in her. His grin deepened.

She assessed this stranger. Handsome. Holding himself with strength and confidence. She'd already noted his dark eyes and how they probed. Realizing she stared, she looked away. "Sorry," she gulped and slowly brought her gaze back to his. His wide grin erased the last flickers of annoyance, and she chuckled. "I don't always run full force into strangers. Nor do I usually take out my frustrations on unsuspecting visitors. It's just been that kind of day. I apologize."

He touched the brim of his hat. "Not a problem. We all have our share of troubles these days."

"Far too true." If she didn't take care of Mrs. Crebs, her difficulties would multiply several times. She tore her gaze away from the stranger and paused. "Are you staying in town?" Heat stung her eyes at the boldness of her question. Quickly, she added, "If so, welcome." She fled with her embarrassment. Now the man would think her both cranky and a dolt.

Her feet slowed as the Crebses' house came into view. *Lord, help me be gracious. Help Mrs. Crebs be charitable and give me another chance.* She sucked in a deep breath that did little to calm her nerves, and knocked on the back door.

Mrs. Crebs yanked it open as if she'd been waiting for Madge. Madge knew she would have been staring at the big clock hanging on the wall and clacking her fingernails against the table as she waited. "You're late again. It's inexcusable." Then she saw her laundry and shrieked.

Madge grimaced at the shrill sound, then hurried to explain. "I had an accident. I'm sorry. I'll take everything home and do it over. I promise it will be spotless."

Mrs. Crebs snatched articles from Madge. "You've ruined my best tablecloth."

"I'll fix it." She would fall on her knees and beg for another chance if it would do any good.

"Don't bother. I've given you more than enough chances. I'll find someone else. Someone I can trust. I've never heard of the Chinaman dumping laundry in the dirt."

The door slammed in Madge's face. Mrs. Crebs, with her five children, had been Madge's best customer. Without the few dollars she made doing the

Crebses' washing, Madge would never scrape together enough for the upcoming mortgage payment.

The future looked bleak.

However, she would not entertain defeat. Somehow, with hard work and perseverance, she would earn the money. *Lord, open up another opportunity for me. Please.*

With no reason to hurry, she didn't dash back to the car. Instead, she went out the back gate and headed for the church to pray. She desperately needed God's help.

Judd Kirk watched the woman rush down the street. That had been an interesting encounter. The first thing he'd noticed about her—aside from the alarm on her face as the stack of linens had tumbled to the ground—had been the mass of wavy brown hair tugged by the wind. Her brown eyes had flashed as if driven by an inner urgency. He recognized the feeling…he'd personally dealt with his own inner force for the past year. She hurried down the street as if chasing after something beyond her reach.

He shifted his stance to study the reason he stood here. The silent house. Obviously still empty. For how long? He'd searched for the man since he'd returned home, as soon as his brother had informed him of the details. This was the closest he'd come to locating him—a house he understood had been rented by the one he sought.

He glanced around. Someone stood at a front gate and called across to a fellow sauntering down the sidewalk. Called him by name. They both watched Judd—noting the stranger in their midst. Golden Prairie was small enough that a fellow hanging about for no apparent reason would attract attention. And speculation. Notice would make him conspicuous and likely alert his prey to his presence.

Not something he needed or wanted. But he intended to stay until he completed his business. Best, however, if he blended into the surroundings.

What he needed was a job allowing him to hang around without raising questions.

Turning, he headed back toward the main street. The storekeeper would know what work was available, preferably out of town yet close enough to allow him to watch this place.

He clumped along the wooden sidewalk and stepped into the store. Dust hung in the air. The scent of leather and coal stung his nostrils. The shelves carried a good array of canned and dry goods. But the whole place held an air of defeat—much like the land around him. And its occupants. "Afternoon."

"Uh-huh." The bespectacled man nodded and gave him a long, unblinking study. "You another of Mrs. Morgan's prospects?"

Judd had no idea what the man meant, but it seemed a trail that might lead somewhere. He would follow it and see. "Could be."

"Well, you ain't the first. In fact—" He tipped his head and seemed to count something on the inside of his eyelids. "Lesse, a young fella went out just a bit ago. He was number four. I guess that makes you number five."

"Seems a lot." But he didn't know what they were talking about, so he had no idea if it was or not. Perhaps, with a little leading, the storekeeper would spare the information.

"Mrs. Morgan is a mite particular, especially concerning her eldest daughter, Miss Louisa. Frail she is. Not like Miss Madge. There she goes now." He nodded toward the window at a vehicle chugging along, coughing and complaining.

In the car sat the young woman who, a short while ago, had steamed into Judd. Madge, the man said. Madge Morgan. Somehow the name suited her. Determined despite disagreeable odds.

The storekeeper languidly continued. "Now, there's a hard worker. Ain't nothing goin' to stop her. No, siree. That gal has been fighting for a decent livelihood since Mr. Morgan died. Doin' mighty fine, too."

Judd followed the car's erratic passage past the store. A fighter. And pretty, too. He brought his attention back to the information the storekeeper had hinted at. "What's Mrs. Morgan looking for in particular?"

"Just what it says in the advertisement. Here it is if you need to refresh your memory." He pointed to a newspaper clipping tacked by the cash register. "Don't think she wanted us to know what she was up to but my brother found the ad in the city paper and sent me a copy."

Judd leaned over to read:

WANTED: A GOOD MAN TO TEACH INVALID LADY FINER ASPECTS OF LANGUAGES AND ARTS. ROOM AND BOARD IN EXCHANGE FOR LESSONS. MUST BE A TRUE GENTLEMAN.

"A tutor?" Never expected that.

"Miss Louisa's interested in learning."

"How old is Miss Louisa?"

"Well, lessee. I think Miss Madge must be eighteen now, though she has more smarts than many twice her age. I guess that would make Miss Louisa nineteen. The three girls are pretty close in age."

"Three?"

"Yup. There's Sally, too. Guessin' she's seventeen. Miss Louisa's the prettiest, but in my opinion, Miss Madge, now she's the one a man should consider. Why, if I was twenty years younger…"

Judd stared as the man's voice trailed off and red crept up his neck before he cleared his throat and shifted away.

"You say there's been plenty of interest in the job."

"Mrs. Morgan is particular. Hey, lookee, there's number four now. Maybe ask him how it went."

"I guess I might." In private. He left the store, strode toward the approaching car and signaled the man to stop. "Hear you were out to the Morgan place."

"Indeed I was. A most promising situation. I didn't meet Miss Morgan, but I understand she is frail but eager with a goodly desire to learn. I believe her interests lean toward art history and literature, though I'm certain with a little guidance she will develop an equal keenness for science and Latin." He rubbed his hands together in anticipation. "The mother is overprotective, which might pose a handicap, but I believe I could have success in overcoming that." He sat up straighter, though he was small, so his effort to look important lacked impact.

"Well, good luck to you." Judd stepped back and assessed the information as the man drove away. His years in university might prove productive after all, even if he hadn't pursued being a teacher.

Yes, indeed, this job would serve his purposes very well.

* * *

A week later Madge sang as she hung another batch of laundry. Father had had no idea how the big room upstairs would be used, strung now with row after row of lines, providing a place to dry things away from the invading dust carried by the relentless winds buffeting the house and all God's creatures.

It was her number one selling point in her offer to do laundry for others—the promise of sparkling white linens. The only way she could guarantee that was by hanging them indoors, out of the dust-laden wind.

She finished pegging the sheet on the line, removed the earlier items, now dry, and started ironing. Her pet cat, Macat, who kept her company as she worked, settled on the nearby stool and began a grooming ritual.

Doing laundry day after day was hard, relentless work, but it was satisfying to produce stacks of fresh sheets and crisp shirts she delivered in town to those people who still had money to pay for her services. Thank God for the few who seemed unaffected by the Depression. The coins she earned slowly collected in the old coffee can downstairs.

Through the open window she watched Sally dump the bucket of kitchen scraps to the chickens, then pause to look around. Her younger sister was quiet and content. Louisa, her older sister, seemed satisfied with her life, as well. Madge was the one with a restless drive to get things done. Without Madge's constant prodding and working, the others might be lulled into complacency until the house was taken from them, never letting the specter of being homeless cross their minds. Even Mother's concern didn't match Madge's determination that the family not end up in such a state.

Madge had managed to persuade one more lady to let her do part of her laundry—only the sheets and table linens, which she hesitated to hang out in the dust. Madge appreciated the job but it didn't make up for the loss of wages her work for Mrs. Crebs had brought in.

As she folded items, she muttered to Macat, who watched her every move. "It's going to be close." In fact, too close for comfort after having been forced to buy a new tire for the car. She clattered down the stairs, Macat meowing at her heels. She ignored the cat's demands, paused on her way through the kitchen to say hello to Sally, who sat surrounded by the mending, and Louisa in her lounge chair reading, with her little dog, Mouse, curled on her lap.

Madge hurried to the front room and Father's desk. She opened the drop lid, scooped up the coffee can, sat down and slowly counted the change and few bills. Her cheeks grew taut, and she felt the heat seep from them. "It's not all here." She couldn't believe it. Who would steal from their savings?

She scooped up Macat and held her close, comforting herself in the silky fur.

Mother paused at the doorway. "Madge?"

Madge struggled to form a thought. A word. "The money. Missing. Stolen."

Mother slipped into the room and closed the door behind her. She patted Madge's shoulder. "It's okay. I took it. I meant to tell you but I—"

"Took it? Why?"

Mother glanced around to make sure they were alone, then whispered. "For Louisa."

"More medicine?" Madge wouldn't resent the expense. Louisa had had pneumonia a number of times. The disease left her lungs weak and required all of them to guard her health. Sometimes it seemed, no matter how hard Madge worked, Louisa's illness ate up way too much of the money. Or the car bit into their savings—though she had figured out how to fix tires on her own, how to adjust the throttle and choke and how to wire things together in hopes they would limp through a few more days. She wished they still had a horse so she could resort to using a wagon. Mentally, she put it on the list. Perhaps someone would trade a horse for her labors. Then she'd need to figure out a way to get enough hay for another animal. She kept her attention on scratching

Macat behind the ears, afraid Mother would see her worry and frustration if she lifted her head.

"Not medicine, dear."

"Then what?" Medicine she understood. What else could there be? Though Mother had a habit of underestimating the expenses and the limited resources for earning money. Father had always protected Mother from the harsh realities of life, so even in these hard times, Mother remained optimistic, always believing things would somehow, as if by magic, fix themselves.

"I want to help Louisa find a husband."

"You bought a man?" Madge couldn't decide if she was more intrigued or shocked. How did one go about purchasing a man? How much did it cost? Did you get to select size, color, style? Her thoughts flitted unexpectedly to the man she had bumped into in town. She blinked away the memory of black eyes and dark hair and returned to considering Mother's announcement.

If one bought a man, was there a money-back guarantee?

Mother pulled a clipping from her pocket and hesitated. "You must promise not to say anything."

"Certainly." Her curiosity grew to overwhelming proportions.

Mother unfolded the scrap of paper and handed it to her. "I placed this ad in a paper."

Madge read the notice. Then she read it again. Mother had advertised for a teacher for Louisa. "It says nothing about marriage."

Mother sat in Father's chair—a sure sign of her mental state. Madge watched her closely. Was she hiding something?

"You know there are no eligible young men around. Most of them are in relief camps."

Madge nodded. The government had created camps for the unemployed young men where they built roads, cut trees and did a number of labor jobs. The idea of work camps was fine. Give young men a place to sleep, food to eat and a job. Get them off the streets. But to her thinking, it only hid the problem. She bit her tongue to keep from saying what she thought of many of the prime minister's political moves. Surely a smart man, a man from their own province even, could do something to stop this horrible decline.

Mother continued. "The rest are riding the rails, hoping to find a job somewhere or trying to avoid the relief camps." She sighed long and hard. "I simply can't stand by and let Louisa turn into an old maid, having to depend on her sisters to take care of her as she gets older."

"Ma, she's only nineteen." She smiled as Macat jerked her head up and meowed as if agreeing with her.

"I was married and had her by that age."

"I know." Those were different times. Mother knew as well as anyone. No point in reminding her. "So the money…?"

"I used it to buy the ad for a tutor."

"You actually found someone?"

"I did. A very nice man who starts today."

Madge opened her mouth. Shut it with an audible click. Tried again. "You did all this behind my back?"

Mother smiled gently. "I felt I had to do something. I know we need the money for the payment, but I thought the wages from Mrs. Crebs and the other jobs you've picked up would be enough." She paused a beat. "On my part, I can cut down on expenses. We don't need meat as often as we've been eating it. We'll trust God to provide and do our best to live wisely." Her look begged Madge to understand.

None of them had expected Mrs. Crebs to be so miffed.

She squeezed Mother's hands. "And this man you hired?"

"He seems ideal for Louisa—gentle, well-educated…. I know I can count on you to do everything you can to help me in this. But please don't say anything to Louisa about my ulterior motives. You know how offended she'd be."

Madge nodded, even though she felt as if she had hung her sister from a tree to be plucked like ripe fruit. "You're sure he's a good gentleman?"

"If he's not, I will personally run him off the place with a hot poker."

Madge chuckled at the sudden spurt of spunk her mother revealed. Sometimes she suspected she and Mother were more alike than Mother cared to confess. "I'll do what I can to help the cause, but if I suspect he's not suitable, I will be right at your side with another hot poker."

The two of them laughed. Mother patted Madge's hand. "I can always count on you." Her expression faltered. "However, I didn't expect my decision would come at such a bad time."

Madge couldn't bear to have her mother worried. "I'm sure things will work out." She wouldn't burden her mother with the fear rippling up her spine.

Mother nodded, accepting Madge's reassurance. "Now I best get back to the kitchen before the girls wonder what we're up to. By the way, the gentleman arrives this afternoon."

Madge waited for her departure, then studied the funds in the can. How was she to pay the mortgage? She'd have to find another job, earn more money, perhaps speak to the banker about a few days' grace. She rubbed the back of her neck. Where was she going to find someone willing and able to pay for any kind of work?

Lord, I can't help but worry. The idea of the four of us being out on the street is enough to cause me concern. Lord, it's beyond me to see how to fix this. However, I know You are in control. Please send an answer my way before we lose our house.

Maybe this tutor, poor unsuspecting man, might offer a future for Louisa. Madge giggled, picturing him. No doubt gray-haired and asthmatic. But Louisa would never pay a mind to such things so long as he was attentive and educated. She paused to pray he was everything Mother expected before she returned the can to the desk and closed the drop lid. Time to return to washing and ironing. She sat Macat on the floor and headed back upstairs with her pet purring at her heels.

A while later, dinner over, she hung about waiting for the arrival of the expected man.

Louisa had primped and put on her best dress. She had gathered up her favorite books. "I'm going to ask him if he's read these. That way I'll know what we can talk about."

Madge never quite understood Louisa's fascination with books and ideas. Since she was small, Madge preferred to be outdoors. It turned out to be a good thing she'd followed her father relentlessly, begging to help. After his death three years ago, she stepped into his role and took care of the chores and so much more. They'd had to let most of the land go, but Madge had insisted they must keep enough for a milk cow and her calf. Again, she wished she'd kept a horse, as well. But looking back was useless.

Sally shoved aside the stockings she had been carefully darning. "I'm going to the garden to see if I can find any greens left after that last blow."

Mother stopped her. "Sally, I want you to meet this man first."

Sally sat back down with a soft sigh. Madge wanted to make her face life squarely. Why was Sally so shy? Seemed Madge had gotten too much boldness and Sally none.

"Very well, Mother," Sally murmured, twisting her hands and looking so miserable Madge had to quell her frustration. At least Mother didn't relent and let her go, as she often did.

Mother pulled aside the curtain. "He's coming." She sat down and feigned disinterest.

Not prepared to pretend she wasn't filled with curiosity, Madge planted herself in front of the window. Macat climbed to the ledge to join her. "He's driving a Mercedes Roadster. About a 1929 model, if I'm not mistaken. Makes our old Model A look as pathetic as it is. He must have washed his car before he left town."

"Madge, get away from the window. He'll think we're spying."

"Mother, I am spying. And if he thinks we shouldn't be interested, well… He's getting out now." She laughed aloud. "And he's wiping the dust from the fenders. If he figures to keep his pretty car dust free he'll have a full-time job."

Louisa hissed. "Madge, stop staring. He'll think we have no manners."

"No. He'll think I have no manners. You'd never give him reason to think it of you."

Louisa giggled.

Madge didn't have to look to know her pretty sister had blushed becomingly. Everything Louisa did was pretty and becoming.

"I couldn't stand to work with a man who wasn't clean and tidy," Louisa said.

"Well, this one is downright fastidious. And he's headed this way." Madge turned from the window. But only to move toward the door to invite the man in. And give him a good once-over before she allowed him to spend time with her older sister.

She waited for the knock, then pulled the door open. The man before her sported a beard. His hair was short and tamed. His dusty suit hung on his body as if he'd recently lost weight. His subdued coloring supported the idea. He seemed faintly familiar. As she stared, he turned away and coughed.

"Excuse me, ma'am. I'm here to tutor Miss Louisa."

"Have we met before?"

He shook his head. "I don't think so."

"Didn't I run into you on the sidewalk a week ago? Literally."

"Ma'am. I'm sure I would recall such a thing."

She stared into dark eyes. They no longer probed, but she would never forget them. Yet no flicker of recognition echoed in the man's face.

Could she be mistaken? She tried to recall every detail of the encounter. Certainly this man looked tidier, wore schoolteacher clothes, and slouched—but the eyes. How could she be confused about them?

She hesitated, not yet inviting him in. What reason would he have for pretending she hadn't seen him before? And why did her heart feel shipwrecked at the idea of Mother choosing this man for Louisa?

Madge sucked in bracing air, straightened her shoulders and stepped back. She was not one to entertain fanciful ideas. Not Madge Morgan, who was practical to the core.

"Please, come in." Whoever he was, whatever he hid, she'd watch him so keenly he'd never succeed in doing anything but what he was meant to do—tutor Louisa.

Chapter Two

Judd knew she recognized him, but it was imperative he remain incognito. He'd grown his beard, cut his hair and changed his appearance as much as possible. He'd even found a suit coat that hung on him, hoping to persuade anyone who cared to notice that he'd lost a lot of weight. Of necessity he would give a false name, for if his prey heard his real one, he might suspect something. He did not want the man warned and cautious.

Mrs. Morgan joined her daughter. "Madge, this is the man I told you is to tutor Louisa. Justin Bellamy. Please come in, Mr. Bellamy."

Judd limped into the room. He figured a lame leg and poor lungs would complete his disguise.

He immediately saw the young woman who would be his pupil. A chinalike beauty in a pale pink dress sat beside a table laden with textbooks and sketch paper. A small white dog with black spots sat on her lap, studying Judd with interest. He figured Louisa's hands on the dog's back persuaded the animal not to go into attack mode. Though the dog would offer little threat.

"My daughter, Louisa."

Judd bowed. "Ma'am, I understand you're interested in furthering your education."

Louisa smiled—sweet and gentle—a marked contrast to the decisive study from Madge, who followed him across the room like a cat watching a pigeon, waiting for the right time to pounce.

He sucked in air and remembered to slouch as if it hurt to walk. She could play guard cat all she wanted. He refused to have his feathers ruffled.

As if to reinforce Judd's feeling of being stalked, a big gray cat jumped from the window ledge and sauntered over to examine the toes of his boots.

Louisa spoke, drawing his attention back to her. "I'd love to go to university. Unfortunately..." She trailed off, but he understood the many things she didn't say. It was too costly. Her health wouldn't allow it. It simply wasn't practical. But she was fortunate her mother cared enough about her thirst for knowledge to hire a tutor. He would do what he could to satisfy her.

"It's a stimulating environment. I'll do my best to share some of what I learned."

She leaned forward, eagerness pouring from her in waves. "I especially want to learn the history of the great artists. And if you would be so good as to…" Her voice fell to a whisper. "Tell me what it's like to be surrounded by so much learning, so much knowledge." As if uncomfortable with her burst of enthusiasm, she ducked her head, but not before he'd seen the flood of pink staining her cheeks.

"I'll do my very best."

To his left he could feel Madge building up a boiler full of steam.

Mrs. Morgan saved them both from the explosion he feared would sear the skin off him. "This is my youngest daughter, Sally."

Judd turned, noticed for the first time the younger girl shrinking back against her chair at the far side of the table.

Her gaze darted to him and away. Then she lifted her head and gave him a sweet smile. "Welcome, Mr. Bellamy."

"Justin, please." He'd never remember he was Mr. Bellamy, but at least Justin started the same as Judd, which is why he'd chosen the name. He remembered to cough as he glanced around the circle of women. Madge's gaze waited, hot and demanding. He gave his most innocuous look, rounding his eyes in faux innocence.

"I'll show you to your quarters," Madge said, her voice full of warning. "Then you can get to work."

"Yes, ma'am."

She pulled her lips into a terse expression, and her eyes narrowed before she spun around.

He followed her swift stride outside, his own pace slow and measured, though he fought an urge to march to her side and match her step for step. As the wind blasted him in the face, he gave a cough for good measure.

She waited by his car. "Get your things and follow me. It's just across the yard."

Mrs. Morgan had said he'd have his own private quarters when he spoke to her in town, having arranged an interview there. Another reason to convince him he wanted this job. He would be able to slip in and out unnoticed as he tracked his foe.

He followed her to a tiny house—one small window, a narrow door and a low roof. She opened the door and stepped inside with him at her heels. Only the wall facing the yard was boards. The others were sod. "It's a—"

"A soddie. Yes. The original house. I hope you'll be comfortable." The tone of her voice suggested she wished anything but. "The bed's made up. There're shelves for your belongings."

She'd been waving at things as she talked but now spun on him. Her gaze raked him. "I know you're the

man I saw before. If you're up to no good, I'll soon
enough find out."

"Miss Madge, you must be mistake—"

"Don't Miss Madge me, Justin Bellamy. What-
ever your scheme, I'll not let you harm my family."
She marched for the door—all of three steps away.
"You'll be taking meals with us. Supper is at six,
which gives you time to earn your keep by teaching
Louisa something she wants to learn."

Judd watched her until she slammed into the
house. Her suspicions were going to make his stay
complicated, but he'd simply have to be extra cautious. He hated being dishonest, but he didn't have
much choice.

He recalled Madge's anger when she'd plowed
into him on the sidewalk. Remembered how she'd
relented and chuckled. Too bad she couldn't find
humor in this situation. He'd love to hear her laugh
again, see her eyes flash with amusement.

He flung his bag on the bed. He was not here to
let pretty brown eyes confuse him. On the surface
he was here to teach Louisa history and other sub-
jects.

His real reason, however, would never take second
place to his job. And if he felt any tug of regret that
his dishonesty made an enemy out of Madge, he
firmly ignored it.

* * *

Madge returned to the house. She'd been churning out clean sheets all morning and hauling them upstairs to hang and dry. She still had two more tubs to do, but she welcomed the chance to stomp up and down the stairs, huffing and puffing. Macat, sensing her mistress's mood, climbed to her perch on the stool and observed with narrowed eyes.

"I'll keep this to myself," she muttered to the cat. "No need to worry Mother or Sally or frighten Louisa, but that man is hiding something."

But what? And why did it make her so cross?

She hated herself for denying the truth and even more for admitting it, but since she'd bumped into him a week ago, she'd thought of him once or twice—dark, intense eyes full of honesty. Or so she'd believed. She snorted. "Honest, indeed. That man is lying through his teeth."

But then, so was she. Thought of him once or twice? Ha. But she did not want to admit the truth... He came to her mind almost constantly.

She pretended she didn't notice him return from the cabin with two books under his arm. Instead, she rushed upstairs with the last load of wet laundry, and muttered protests as she hung the sheets.

Only when she was certain he would be ensconced in the front room with Louisa did she clatter down the stairs, rushing past the doorway without allowing herself to glance in. Macat followed at a leisurely pace, protesting Madge's haste.

Madge's emotions gave strength to her muscles, and she carried the wash water, two buckets at a time, to the garden where she rationed a drink to the few surviving plants. Whatever they raised was essential for providing adequate food, so she'd constructed wooden windbreaks around the plants in the hopes of nursing them through the dust storms and drought. Still, they didn't promise more than a bit of cabbage or a few scrawny potatoes.

She drove off the grasshoppers, only to watch hordes more replace them.

She paused from her labors to glance toward the heavens. *God, You see our situation and that of so many people. Please send relief. And make it possible for me to find more paying work or some source of income.*

Trusting God was difficult when the circumstances offered nothing but failure. But as long as she could remember, she'd made it a practice to trust Him. She never doubted His love. It was as solid as the Rock of Gibraltar—as Father had always said. His love surely meant He would meet their needs. Having a home seemed pretty essential to her, especially given that they had no male protection and Louisa was frail.

She drew in a deep breath and settled her assurance on God's provision before she returned to the washtubs and turned them over to dry. Until tomorrow, when she would begin another stack of laundry.

Finished with that part of the task, she stepped inside and paused to watch Louisa and Justin bent over a book. Harrumph. She knew he was hiding something.

Louisa glanced up, a glitter of pleasure in her eyes.

Instantly, guilt flooded Madge's lungs. Mother had approved this man. Decided he was an appropriate candidate for Louisa. Seeing Louisa's enjoyment after an hour shamed Madge. She had no reason to be so distrustful or so—

Lord, help me. Not only am I suspicious, but I am annoyed because I saw him first. Unless he has a stronger twin.

She could always hope.

By the time Madge had finished ironing and taken care of a few outdoor chores, Sally announced supper. Madge had decided to give Justin the benefit of the doubt until she had something more solid than a chance encounter on the street to base her suspicions on.

Mother and Sally had the meal almost ready, but Madge helped place the serving dishes on the table. She noted with a mixture of gratitude and annoyance that the extra plate had been placed besides Louisa's, which put Justin across from her. Not that it mattered where he sat, but perhaps this was the best place for him. From this position she could steal glances at him, perhaps catch something in his eyes he couldn't hide.

Besides the dark intensity she recalled.

Mother announced the meal was served, and they sat around the table, Justin taking the indicated spot. Knowing her expression would give away things she didn't want known—like interest and regret—she kept her head lowered until Mother said the blessing.

For a few minutes they were busy passing food. Somehow Mother and Sally managed to make their meager supplies stretch to satisfying meals. Tonight the hunk of meat she'd received in lieu of wages from one of her customers had been ground and mysterious ingredients added until it looked generous and succulent. The aroma had teased her taste buds for the past hour. Sally had managed to scrounge enough lamb's quarters for rich greens and had stolen new potatoes from under the plants in the garden. Two small, tasty nuggets each. Now, with a man sharing meals, they would have to make food go further. Justin Bellamy had better prove his worth.

Madge had almost balked at accepting the meat instead of getting the cash she needed, but tonight she was grateful for good food.

"This is wonderful," Justin said. "I haven't eaten this well in months."

"You can credit Sally with her inventiveness," Mother said.

Justin turned to Sally. "Thank you, Miss Sally."

Sally ducked her head. Always so painfully shy. Madge supposed it came from being the youngest. Then she flashed Justin a bright smile. "You're welcome."

Madge studied Justin, assessing his reaction to Sally's gratitude. But he only gave a slight smile and a quick nod. Then, before she could look away, his gaze shot to her. "You have a very nice home."

She nodded. "No need to sound surprised."

"Madge!" Mother scolded.

But Justin laughed. "I'm not at all surprised."

Did she detect a hint of acknowledgement? As if admitting they'd met earlier?

"Tell me more about yourselves." He held Madge's gaze a moment longer, then shifted to include the others. "How long have you lived here?"

Madge held her tongue for almost a second, but she burst with insistent curiosity and the words poured forth. "Surely you and Louisa have discussed this." After all, they had sat almost head to head, undisturbed, all afternoon. A little sting of jealousy shocked her. She couldn't resent the time he spent with Louisa. That's why he was here.

"No. It's been strictly business."

Louisa blushed. "He told me of the first day in college when there are get-acquainted parties. He says within a few days it's easy to tell those who want to learn from those who only want to have fun. Or freedom from parental control." She drew in a rough breath. "I can't imagine wasting such an opportunity." Her sigh was long and shaky.

Madge stuffed back any remnants of resentment. She'd always been able to do what she wanted—work, run, play, ride—whereas Louisa's activities had been shaped by her weak lungs. She must not resent any scraps of happiness her sister found.

Not even if they involved a man like Justin—a man about whom she held suspicions and a lurking sense of something else, which would remain nameless and denied.

Mother took on the job of telling Justin about the family. "We moved here from the city of Edmonton six years ago. My husband wanted to farm. We bought this place and built a new house." She sighed. "In hindsight, perhaps we should have been satisfied with something much smaller, but at the time the economy was so bright. My husband died unexpectedly three years ago—just before the crash. At least he was spared that."

Somehow Madge didn't think Father would be as glad as Mother seemed to think. He'd surely have wanted to shepherd them through this crisis, see they were safe and sheltered. They needed him now like never before. But obviously the Lord thought otherwise.

"I'm sorry for your loss. I'm sure it's been tough to manage."

Justin sounded as if Mother's loss really mattered to him. Did he understand how hard life was? Truly, without assurance that God would take care of them, there were times Madge wondered how they would make it through another month.

"The situation is difficult for everyone. We are perhaps more fortunate than some," Mother said.

"How's that?"

Madge continued to study him, drawn inexorably by the gentle concern in his voice. Their gazes touched, and he held the look for a moment before sliding away, leaving her feeling washed and exposed. She must guard her thoughts better, lest he guess at her confusion of interest and caution.

Mother spoke her name, and Madge shifted her attention to hear her words. "Madge has kept us all afloat."

Madge revealed nothing in her expression. None of the agony some of her decisions had caused as Mother explained how she'd negotiated a deal to give the bulk of their land to the bank in exchange for keeping the house and a mortgage they could manage. She might soon be forced to admit it was too much if God didn't provide an answer to her prayer for another job, another source of income.

After a few minutes she interrupted the discussion. "It's your turn. Tell us about your family and where you're from."

Judd hauled his thoughts to a halt. He didn't want the conversation focused on him. He'd tried to plan what he could reveal and what he must hide. Figured he had it worked out satisfactorily, but still he didn't like the thought of having to tell half-truths in order to keep his identity a secret. Besides, he'd enjoyed hearing how Madge managed to save their home. And not just save the home to live like paupers. These people ate decently and were together. Not everyone could claim such success.

His jaw tightened. His own mother could testify to that, but it wasn't her fault things had turned out as they had.

Four pairs of eyes silently urged him to share. One pair, especially, challenged him. He'd tried to divide his attention equally among those at the table, but again and again, his gaze left the others to watch Madge. She wore a practical brown dress. Her glistening brown hair tumbled about as if it had a mind of its own.

Aware they waited for his answer, he pulled his

thoughts back from concentrating on Madge. "My mother is a widow, too. She's had a difficult time because of the reversal of her fortunes."

Mrs. Morgan sighed. "The crash hit so many people. Now the drought is touching even those who had no money to lose in the first place. On top of that, the low prices for our products...why, wheat is down to twenty-eight cents a bushel. How can farmers hope to survive?"

They all shook their heads. He let them think his mother had lost everything in the collapse of the financial markets. Only in her case, it was a scoundrel who'd brought about her personal crash.

Mrs. Morgan continued. "At least she has you to help."

"And three more sons."

"Four boys?" Mrs. Morgan perked up.

He wondered if she regretted having only daughters.

"I expect your mother is well taken care of."

"She is now." Shoot. He shouldn't have said "now." Four pairs of eyebrows shot upwards, and four pairs of eyes demanded an explanation. Aware of an especially intense gaze from across the table, he turned to Mrs. Morgan, afraid his emotions might reveal themselves despite his best intentions. Could he explain without giving away more than was safe? "We didn't realize how badly she needed help. She had too much pride to confess it. Somehow she managed to hide it even from Levi, who is still living at home."

"Tell us about your brothers. Is Levi the youngest?"

"Yes. He's seventeen. Redford is the next one. He's teaching. Has been for…well, he's twenty-three, so I guess he's been teaching four years now. Then Carson is a lawyer. He's a year younger than I am."

"How old would that make him?" Madge demanded.

Judd tucked away a smile. Curious about him, was she? Even though she watched him with as much concentration as did Louisa's small dog. "Carson is twenty-five."

They studied each other across the table, measuring, assessing. He wished he didn't have to conceal the truth about who he was. But he did. Determination stiffened his muscles, making his mouth tighten.

Her eyes narrowed. "How did you hurt your leg?"

"Madge!" Mrs. Morgan sounded as if she couldn't believe her daughter, though whether because her question was so bold or because of the hint of mockery in her voice.

"I got thrown from a wild horse." At least that part was true.

Louisa gasped. "A wild horse? Why would you be riding such a creature?"

"My job was to break him. I decided to do it the fast way. Only it proved to be the slow way for me. Someone else had to finish the job while I lay around recuperating." Again, that part was true.

Madge squinted at him. "I thought you were a teacher. Isn't that why you went to university?"

He chuckled, pleased he confounded her with the truth. "After a year of teaching I realized I didn't really like the job, so I let Redford apply for the position and I headed to the foothills. That's where I was when my mother lost her home." If he'd been around, he might have seen what was happening. Perhaps been able to stop it.

Instead, he'd been away, unaware of events, but he aimed to right things as best he could now. The man responsible for his mother's loss would not escape without somehow paying. Judd didn't much care how, so long as he paid. He'd watch the man, see what he planned, who he picked for his next victim, then confront him, expose him to one and all, make him own the truth and then turn him over to the law. He wondered if the courts would make him repay his victims. Sometimes he considered taking the law into his own hands but so far had listened to the voice of reason—or moderation, perhaps—drilled into him by his mother.

"Where is your mother living now?"

Mrs. Morgan's question pulled him back to the

watchful interest of Madge and the quiet curiosity of her sisters. "Mother and Levi found a good home with Carson in Regina, Saskatchewan."

"I'm glad. It must be a relief for her."

"And me."

Mrs. Morgan's gaze softened. "Your mother is blessed to have sons who care about her."

"She's doubly blessed. Her faith has never faltered. She's certain God will take care of her no matter what." She'd repeated the words over and over as she tried to make Judd understand the man who stole her money shouldn't be hunted down and tied to a fence to dry. "'God,' she'd said, 'is in control. He will see to justice.'"

"As do I," Mrs. Morgan said. "Girls, I want to assure you I interviewed Justin at length about his faith, and he convinced me he is a strong believer."

At her faith in him, guilt burned up Judd's throat. He certainly believed in God, had become a Christian when he was only eight, but he wasn't willing to sit back and wait for God to take care of things that were in his power to deal with. Like the man who stole his mother's life savings.

"Where were you when you broke your leg?" Madge sounded like Carson with his best lawyer voice. Her question was more than a question; it was a demand for an explanation.

"On a ranch in the foothills of Alberta."

"A cowboy." She sounded as if that explained everything.

His heart fell as he realized his words verified her suspicions about meeting him on the street a week ago when he'd been dressed as a cowboy rather than a teacher. In hindsight, it might have been better to disguise that fact. But it was too late now. Somehow he had to convince her—all of them—he was no longer a cowboy. He shrugged and remembered to cough. "It seemed like a good idea at the time, but it's not as romantic and adventuresome as one might think. It's mostly hard, unrelenting work that wears many a man down to the bone." He spoke the truth—a relief to his burning conscience, though it wasn't an opinion he shared.

"Wouldn't the fresh air be good for your lungs?" Madge asked, her voice signaling a touch of disbelief.

"Madge, I'm sure Justin doesn't care to have his health problems as part of our conversation."

Madge gave her mother an apologetic smile, then fixed Judd with an uncompromising look. He didn't claim any special powers at reading a woman's mind, but he got her loud and clear. She silently warned him she would be challenging everything he said and did.

He would have to guard his words and steps carefully.

She pulled her gaze away and pushed back from the table. "It's getting late. I've lingered too long. Sally, Mother, do you mind if I don't assist with dishes tonight? I still have to get the cow and calf home and milk the cow. I have laundry to deliver to two customers as well as pickup for tomorrow's customers."

"I'll help you." Judd pushed back, then remembered his frail health and struggled with getting his breath. He'd watched her pack heavy baskets of wet laundry up the stairs. Fought an urge to assist as she'd emptied the tubs.

"No need."

Louisa released a sigh, causing Judd to think she'd been holding her breath for a long time. "I wondered if we could do more lessons tonight."

"Louisa, I don't want you overtaxed," Mrs. Morgan said. "Besides, I told Justin he would have the evenings to do as he wished."

"Of course, Mother."

Judd already realized how hungry Louisa was to learn. If the students he'd had in school had been half as eager, he might have found teaching a little more rewarding. But even then it wouldn't have satisfied his love of wide-open spaces. Ranching had called to him. It was still in his blood. As soon as he finished with this other business, he'd head west again and perhaps find a place where he could start his own little ranch.

"I don't need help." Madge interrupted his thoughts. "But you're welcome to accompany me. I could show you around a bit."

The warning in her eyes let him know she had more in mind than friendly welcome. His lungs twisted with anticipation.

Mental dueling with Miss Madge might prove to be a lot of fun.

Chapter Three

"Where are we going?" Justin asked as he limped along beside her.

Her first thought had been to stride as fast as usual, leaving him to catch up as best he could, but she'd invited him to accompany her for a specific reason—to try to discover who he really was—the cowboy she'd seen on the street or this weak, namby-pamby man who seemed to prefer books to cows and horses. She'd glimpsed eagerness as he'd talked about ranching. Unintentional, she was certain. But it made her more curious. More convinced he hid something. More confused on how she felt about him.

"I'm forced to take the pair wherever I can find something for them to eat, even if it's only weeds, which make the milk taste awful. Louisa needs the nourishment."

"How do you plan to feed them through the winter?"

The question was continually on her mind. "I've kept the calf for butcher." Feeding another animal strained her resources, but if she could provide adequate food for the family... "I hope I can trade some of the meat for winter fodder."

"Though if no one has any feed..."

She knew as well as he how scarce hay would be. "Perhaps we can get some shipped in."

"Or might be a farmer is giving up and ready to part with what he's scraped together."

"In exchange for cash, which is as hard to find as hay."

They fell into a contemplative silence. Suddenly she realized how easy it had been to talk to him about her problems, how comfortable they'd fit into each other's strides, even with his limp, and how she ached to tell him everything crowding her brain. But she didn't trust him, she didn't want to be attracted to him, and even though she'd seen him first, he was Mother's pick for Louisa. Her protests chased through her thoughts like runaway children. "I must hurry. The cow will be begging to be milked by now." She lengthened her stride, forcing him to step, hop and limp to keep up. She slowed and chuckled.

He caught up to her and coughed a little, though she noted he wasn't out of breath.

"Something funny?" he asked.

"Yes. Us. Look at me. My chin stuck out, rushing across the prairie like I'm trying to outrun a fire, while you hop along like a rabbit with a broken foot. Anyone seeing us would surely shake their head in disbelief." She laughed again, then realized how he might interpret her comments and clamped a hand to her mouth. "I'm so sorry. I didn't mean to mock your limp."

He only laughed, his eyes flashing with amusement. His dark gaze held hers as she gave another nervous laugh. She wasn't sure if she should be embarrassed more by her ill-considered comment, her continuing suspicion or the way her heart lurched as his look invited her into exciting territory full of adventure, excitement and something she couldn't... wouldn't...try to identify—a sense of connection.

She tore her gaze away and forced her steps toward the little slough where she'd found some dried grass for the cow. The cow's desperate lowing reached her, followed by the bleating of the calf. They directed her thoughts sharply back to her responsibilities. She'd tethered them so the calf couldn't suck the cow and steal the precious milk. "The cow needs milking. The calf needs feeding."

"Sounds like a song." He repeated the words, setting them to a rousing camp tune. "And the wind keeps blowing till my mind is numb." He added several more verses, each more mournful than the first, yet comical, and she laughed.

"I see you missed your calling. You should be in the entertainment world."

He grinned, a look so teasing and inviting her mouth went dry. "I don't have a hankering for being pelted with rotten tomatoes when I jest about how hard times are."

She lifted one shoulder in resignation and acknowledgement. "Might as well laugh as cry, I say."

"Amen."

She allowed one brief glance at him. Remnants of his amusement remained, and something more that she recognized as determination—an echo of her own heart. "And do what one can to make things better."

"Exactly."

Her brief glance had gone on longer than she should have allowed. Thankfully they reached the struggling trees at the almost dry slough, and she hurried to release the cow. When she turned to do the same for the calf, Justin already held the rope. Together they headed for home. Usually she had her hands full keeping the calf away from the cow, but with Justin helping it was a lot easier, and they reached the barn in short order.

She turned the cow into the stall. "Do you mind

putting the calf in that pen over there? There's a bit of grain for it."

He did as she asked, then lounged against a post, watching as she milked. Usually she found the time relaxing, but not under his study. "You don't need to stay here."

"See no reason to leave. Unless you want me to."

Did she? Of course she did. Even if she didn't suspect him of something dishonest, even if he was the spotless character Mother seemed to think he was, he held no interest for her. Mother hoped he'd be a match for Louisa.

So why then did she shake her head? "Of course not. Thanks for your help." She returned to the soothing rhythm of milking, as aware of Justin's presence as if he shouted and yodeled rather than waited quietly.

She finished, poured some milk into a trough for the calf and headed for the house to strain the rest for the family. Sally took the pail as she stepped inside.

"I'll take care of this. You go deliver the laundry."

"Thanks."

A few minutes later, Madge sat behind the wheel of their reluctant automobile and tried not to envy Justin his better car. Justin had continued to follow her and, without seeking permission, climbed in beside her. Obviously he meant to accompany her. She couldn't find the strength to suggest otherwise.

Besides—she clung to her excuse—she might discover something about him he didn't mean for her to find.

The clean laundry, smelling of soap and hot irons, sat in neat piles behind them, covered with an old sheet to protect it from the dust.

When they arrived at her first delivery point, he got out and grabbed a basket.

"I can manage. I do all the time."

"Yeah. I guessed that." He led the way up the sidewalk. "You remind me of my mother."

"Should I be insulted to be compared to an older woman or flattered it's your mother?"

He chuckled. "I meant you are independent just like her. She could have let us know she was in trouble, but she didn't. Even when we found out, we practically had to force her to tell us the truth. When the bank foreclosed on her house, she insisted she and Levi could find a place somewhere. It took all of us talking fast and hard to convince her to move in with Carson."

"She sounds like a strong woman." Even as she spoke, Madge shuddered. "I intend to see we don't lose our house. I think Mother and I could manage, but Louisa would suffer ill health from the upset. Who knows what Sally would do? At times she seems ready to conquer any challenge, yet at other times I fear a harsh word will destroy her." Why she was telling him all this left her as puzzled as Sally often did in her reactions to life.

They reached the door, so conversation came to a halt. Madge handed over the clean items and received a few coins. She tucked the money into her deep pocket to add to the coffee can when she got home. The payment was due next week, and she knew without counting she would never make it.

"I need something special to happen," she muttered, then wondered if she'd lost her mind to utter the words aloud.

"What do you mean?"

"Never mind." She eased the automobile down the street to her next delivery. Again, Justin insisted on carrying the basket to the door. Thankfully, the distance was short, making conversation impossible.

She drove three blocks and picked up another batch of laundry.

"Seems to me you're working hard, finding ways to cope. What is it you're worried about?"

She snorted. "We're in a depression. No jobs. No money. Drought. Poor prices. What isn't there to worry about?"

"I hear ya. But not all those things touch each of us personally. For instance, you have work. You have a source of food and your house."

"For now," she muttered, immediately wanting to smack herself for revealing more than she intended.

This wasn't his problem. She didn't even trust him, for goodness' sake. Why would she want to share her problems with him?

"Your house is still mortgaged?"

She grunted. Let him take it for agreement or not. Whatever he wanted. She didn't intend to discuss this with him.

"Are you in danger of losing it?" His quiet words flushed through her, leaving a trickle of anger and determination.

"Not if I have anything to say about it." She took the corner too fast and skidded. Let him think about that instead of talking about losing the house. She couldn't contemplate the possibility. Her anger fled as quickly as it came. "I'm not worried. God has promised to take care of us. I simply have to believe He will." Though it would require divine intervention within the next few days.

"There again, you sound like my mother."

She glanced at him and gave a tight smile that did not budge the determination tightening the skin around her eyes. "She must be a good woman."

He grinned. "I think so." His gaze lingered. Did he think the same of her?

And what difference did it make if he did?

She tried to think of all the reasons it didn't matter, but for a moment, for the space of a heartbeat—for the time it took to blink away from his gaze—she let herself imagine he had complimented her, and she allowed herself to enjoy the thought.

She headed out of town toward the farm. Her journey took her past the Mayerses' place. Young Kenny stood at the end of the garden, a few feet from the edge of the road. She squinted at him. "What's he doing?"

"Best I can guess is he's taking the chickens for a walk."

She sputtered in surprise. "Never heard of walking chickens." But indeed the boy had half a dozen hens tethered by a foot and marched them up and down the end of the garden.

Madge crawled to a halt and leaned out her window. "Kenny, what are you doing?"

"Ma says the chickens have to eat the grasshoppers before they get to the plants." He sounded as mournful as the distant train whistle. "Says I have to keep them here until dark."

"Sounds like a chore."

"It's boring. Stupid chickens wouldn't stay here, so I roped 'em. Now they got nothing to do but chase hoppers." One chicken tore after a hopper to Kenny's right. Two others squawked at the disturbance and flapped in the opposite direction. Kenny had his hands full keeping everything sorted out.

"Well, have fun," Madge called as she drove away. She didn't dare look at Justin until they were well out of Kenny's hearing, then she saw him struggling as much as she was to contain amusement.

They started to laugh. Madge laughed until her stomach felt emptied and her heart refreshed. She gasped for air and dried her eyes. "Never seen that before."

Justin shook his head. "Thought I'd seen every kind of critter that could be led. 'Course, the chickens weren't exactly cooperating, were they? I think poor Kenny is going to end up trussed by his feathered herd."

They burst into fresh gales of laugher as she turned into the yard. The laughter died as they approached the house. She slid a worried look at him. Would he think her silly? But his eyes brimmed with amusement and something as warm as fresh milk, as sweet as clover honey and as forbidden as taking candy from a baby. Yet she couldn't deny the way his glance sought and found a place deep inside where it seemed to fit perfectly.

She tore her gaze away and delivered a firm lecture to herself. Everything about this man was wrong, wrong, wrong. For starters, she knew he was hiding something. Plus, he had been handpicked as a suitable mate for Louisa. What kind of woman would entertain thoughts for a man intended for her sister?

She bolted from the car and reached for the laundry baskets, now full of tumbled, smelly items. But Justin beat her and held them in his arms.

"Where do you want me to put them?"

She nodded toward the coal shed she used as a laundry room. "In there would be fine." She hesitated as he disappeared into the dark interior, then slowly followed, wondering if she didn't step into danger as she crossed the threshold. She grabbed the pull chain, and a bare bulb lit the interior. "On the bench."

He deposited the baskets and looked about, sneezing at the smell of coal dust. "Pretty dingy in here."

"That's why I move everything outdoors unless it's too dusty. Or rainy."

"Rain would be a welcome reason."

"Indeed." The shed was small, and she looked everywhere but at Justin. His closeness pressed at her senses, making her skin warm, filling her lungs with tightness, causing her eyes to sting with embarrassment and pleasure at their recent amusement.

"I enjoyed our little outing."

The softness in his voice pulled her gaze inexorably toward him. His eyes were dark, bottomless, echoing the blackness in the corners of the room. Something about his expression caught at her, held her, joined them in a common thought.

"Especially meeting Kenny and his herd."

A grin started in one corner of her mouth and

worked its way across her face. "If it keeps the grass-hoppers out of the garden, he will surely be in high demand all over the county."

Justin chuckled. "The price of chickens will sky-rocket."

"No one will be able to afford to eat a hen."

"Might put an end to this financial crisis."

They both laughed heartily at their foolishness, but something happened in that shared moment, something Madge would not admit. She could not, would not feel a union of souls beyond anything she had before experienced.

She jerked away. "Thanks for your help and have a good night."

He followed her outside and paused, as if waiting for her to turn and face him. She would not.

"Good night to you, too." He limped toward his quarters.

She headed for the house. Just before she stepped inside, she turned. He paused at his own doorway and glanced back. Her heart jerked in response. He lifted one hand in a little wave. She did the same, struggling to keep her breathing normal, and then ducked inside and quietly closed the door.

"Did you have a good time?" Louisa sat in her lounge chair. Her voice was soft but her eyes hard.

Madge knew her sister didn't care for Justin ac-companying her. Not that she had invited him. Or welcomed him. Or so she tried to convince herself. "I delivered laundry and picked up more. Not exactly a fun occupation."

"What did you talk about?"

She couldn't remember anything except their shared laughter and didn't want to tell Louisa about that. "Huh? Pardon? Who talked about what?"

"You and Justin. You must have said something. After all, you went to town and back. You spent the better part of an hour together."

"I didn't know you would object. Where are Mother and Sally?"

Louisa sighed. "I want to have all his attention. Is that so wrong? He's a good teacher and might turn into a good friend. They're in the living room unraveling an old sweater of Father's."

Guilt clawed at Madge's throat. "I'm sure he'll find you very interesting. You'll soon be the best of friends." He wouldn't be interested in someone like Madge. She was only an old workhorse. Louisa was a graceful swan. "Just be careful. We know very little about him."

Louisa looked ready to argue, then sighed. "It's not like I expect anything but a few lessons from him."

Madge knew Louisa wanted more. And who could blame her? Louisa missed out on a lot of fun because of her health problems, but they had shared confidences all their lives. Louisa dreamed of all the things Madge did—home, love, security. "Do you want help preparing for bed?"

"I can manage." Louisa put Mouse down, and he rushed to the bottom of the stairs where Macat waited. Louisa pushed to her feet.

Madge wrapped her arm about Louisa's waist and held her close. Louisa had been ill so many times. Madge would do anything to protect her. "You mustn't overtire yourself. You'll end up sick. Then you wouldn't be able to study with Justin." She injected a teasing note into her voice and pretended she didn't feel the tiniest ache in her thoughts...her lungs...her heart.

She paused at the front-room door. "Mother, Louisa and I are headed upstairs. Good night."

"We'll finish this before we go up." She spared a brief smile, then turned back to winding yarn as Sally carefully pulled out row after row.

Upstairs, Madge offered again to help, but Louisa insisted she was quite capable of getting to bed on her own. Madge smiled a little at Louisa's faint determination, then retired to her own quarters. Thankfully Father had built the house large enough for the three girls to have their own small rooms. The big room where she hung sheets to dry had been intended as an upstairs parlor for the women when they had company. Mother's room was downstairs off the front room. Madge savored her solitude. She could think and pray and struggle with her wayward thoughts—as she did tonight—without the others knowing.

Louisa had carefully, guardedly, expressed her interest in Justin. And rightfully so. He was perfect for her, as Mother had already seen. At least, if he turned out to be honest he would be. Madge had no right to think of him as anything but Louisa's tutor and, perhaps in the future, Louisa's husband. And her own brother-in-law.

That settled, Madge opened her Bible. She had established a habit of daily reading as a youngster when Father had carefully instructed all of them in the value of such a practice. All three had promised Father they would read at least a few verses every day. Mother continued to remind them of their promise and the value of keeping it. Sometimes Madge mentally excused herself as being too tired, but she'd discovered she found incredible strength and guidance in the Word and comfort in prayer.

She read the chapter where her marker indicated she had quit the night before. The passage was Micah, chapter six. She began to read, got as far as verse eight and stalled. "What doth the Lord require of thee, but to do justly and to love mercy and to walk humbly with thy God?"

Her thoughts smote her, and she bent forward

until her hair fell to the page. Macat thought she wanted to pet her and pushed under her arm, but Madge ignored her. *Oh, Lord, I have forgotten to be humble. I have forgotten mercy and justice. I've been so caught up with fighting my attraction to Justin and in fretting over how I'll pay the mortgage that I've forgotten who You are. I trust You to help me be true and faithful in everything.* Both in her concerns over the needed money and her wayward, unwarranted thoughts about a man who filled her with such nagging doubts. *Lord, show me, reveal to me any secrets he is hiding that might harm us.*

A few minutes later she crawled into bed, her mind at rest, her heart at peace. She would trust God and keep her distance from Justin.

Over the next few days Madge did her best to live up to her decision. Justin kept busy with Louisa. The little bit she saw of them together reinforced her resolve. Louisa's cheeks took on a healthy color. She showed more enthusiasm than she had in a long time. Several times Madge heard her laughter ring out like bells. The sound both seared and cheered her, reminding her of the laughter she'd shared with Justin and, at the same time, reaffirming how perfect he was for Louisa. She caught bits and pieces of conversation between the two as she hurried up and down the stairs. Justin was always so kind and patient with Louisa. In fact, Madge told herself, a perfect match for her. She was happy for Louisa.

If only it was anyone but Justin.

Judd watched Madge hustle up the steps and clenched his teeth. She worked far too hard, packing heavy baskets, carrying buckets of water, delivering the laundry and caring for the cow. Why, he'd even seen her with her head in the bonnet of their old car, adjusting things so it ran.

He wished he could help her, but his job was to teach Louisa, who devoured every bit of information he relayed to her. He'd had to send back home for several more books.

The evening he and Madge had spent together had been enjoyable, but she had pointedly avoided him since. He couldn't help but wonder why. Had he offended her in some way? He intended to find out.

His opportunity came when she began to empty the washtubs. She grabbed her back and stretched as if she hurt. And well she might. The endless work was heavy. "I think I'll help Madge carry away the wash water. She looks tired."

"But—" Louisa ducked her head and swallowed loudly, then her gaze sought her sister and her expression softened. "Of course. To my shame I confess I often take her strength for granted. Yet if something were to happen to her we would all pay an awful price. Go and help her."

"You have this book to study. You're a good student. I feel a fraud trying to teach you. Really, all you need are the books and you could manage on your own."

Bright color stained her cheeks. "How kind of you to say so." She stroked Mouse's back. "But it's because you explain things so well."

He chuckled. "So long as you're happy."

The color in her cheeks deepened. Was she so susceptible to a few kind words? The poor girl needed to get out more, mingle with people. Learn to fight her own battles. Like Madge.

Madge—who seemed set on making it impossible for him to spend time with her.

He hurried out and caught up the pails while her back was turned.

She spun around. Surprise filled her eyes and then, what he hoped was pleasure. The look disappeared so quickly he wondered if he imagined it simply because he wanted it.

"What are you doing?"

"I'll carry the water to the garden."

She faced him, her stance challenging, her expression wary. "Why?"

"You're opposed to a little help?"

"Yes." She hesitated. "No. I just want to know why."

"Hate to see you doing all this hard work by yourself." He dipped the pails into the tub and, ignoring the splashing water, headed for the garden, remembering in time about his limp and cough. He gave two coughs for good measure.

"You're not exactly robust."

He didn't miss the skepticism in her tone and knew she still held suspicions as to who he was—Justin, the crippled teacher, or Judd, the strong cowboy she'd blasted into on the path in town. Not that she'd ever heard his name. Nor had anyone around here. All to his benefit.

Madge found a third bucket, filled it and traipsed after him as if she had to prove she didn't need him.

He paused, caught the glimpse of pain before she hid it. "Your back hurts. If you don't rest, it will only get worse."

She scowled at him, which so delighted him that he laughed and earned himself an even deeper frown. She stomped past him, making sure to slop water on his oxfords.

He laughed again. Madge haughty and annoyed was much better than the Madge who ignored him. His grin remained firmly in place as he followed her. Seeing how she measured out the water to each plant, he did the same. "You should borrow Kenny's trained hens to eat the grasshoppers." He eased his gaze toward her, pleased as could be when her eyes widened and she laughed.

"I'll tell Sally about Kenny. Maybe I can convince her to train her chickens to do the same job."

He emptied the second bucket, and they returned for more water. Questions plagued him, but he waited until they trekked back to the garden to voice them. "Why have you been avoiding me?"

She snorted. "What makes you think I am?"

"Oh, little things. Like waiting until I'm not around to drive off with your deliveries or ducking out of sight when you see me crossing the yard. Or how about the way you race up the steps if I so much as look your direction? I thought after that first evening we might be friends."

"Friends?"

"Is that so hard to picture?" Her reaction stung. Why, lots of young women would be pleased to be friends with him. "Is it because of this?" He slapped his "crippled" leg. "Or this?" He pressed his palm to his chest and coughed. "Am I not good enough for you?"

She stood tall and proud, her expression shocked. "What an awful thing to say. As if I'd judge a person by such standards."

"Exactly what standards would you use?"

"I expect a man to be honest, upright, noble. Have

a sense of humor." Her eyes brightened as if she remembered the laughs they'd shared, then she lowered her head. "But right now all I'm interested in is making sure we have food to eat and a roof over our heads."

He understood that drive. Seeing his mother get justice excluded all else in his thoughts. Or it had until recently, when interest in Madge also took root. "You work far too hard. There must be some other way to get enough to pay your mortgage."

She sniffed. "If you know of something, be sure and let me know. I have three days before my payment is due."

"Will you make it?"

"I'm still waiting for heavenly intervention. If you're concerned, you could pray for me."

He hesitated. She wanted him to pray for her? Did he believe God could provide a stay of execution? He didn't know. For too long he'd depended on his own strength and abilities. It hadn't seemed necessary to call on God for anything.

She headed back for the last of the water. "Sorry I asked."

"No, don't be sorry." He hurried after her, almost forgetting to limp. "I was just trying to think of the last time anyone asked me to pray for them. It's been a while. But it will be an honor to ask God to help you."

She faced him. "Ask and believe."

Slowly he nodded. "I will. I do." Her insistence made it impossible to do otherwise. A strong woman with a strong faith. His respect for her grew.

Her brown eyes flashed. Her brown wavy hair, damp from her hard labor under the glaring sun, was a becoming tangle. Her arms were bare and tanned. In fact, she glowed with health. Even more, her glow revealed an inner beauty of determination and faith.

He forced resistance into his thoughts. He dare not be distracted by her attributes, no matter how appealing she was. He was here under false pretenses, living under an assumed name. She would despise him if she discovered the truth.

He didn't intend she should. There was too much at stake for his real identity to be revealed. Yet it stung to know how she would react if she found out.

Chapter Four

Madge counted the coins again. Still not enough, despite Justin's promise to pray. Perhaps it had been only empty words.

Or maybe she was trusting his prayers more than her God.

Yet neither had produced the necessary help.

She turned to Macat, who sat on the nearby chair, totally disinterested in Madge's problems. "I'll simply have to speak to the banker. He'll surely understand and allow me more time."

She slipped to her room, changed into her best dress, brushed her hair into tidiness and donned a hat she normally saved for church. Intent on looking her best, she powdered her nose. "I look like a farmer with my brown skin."

Macat watched from the comfort of the bed. If cats thought about the actions of humans—and

Madge was certain this one did—they must wonder at all this fuss in the middle of the day. Madge had hurried to get the laundry done earlier than usual. It was ready to deliver while she was in town. "There." She checked her reflection in the mirror. "That's the best I can do. Wish me well." She grabbed her white gloves to pull on before she stepped into the bank.

Macat had nothing to offer but a puzzled meow.

Sucking in air that seemed thin, Madge admitted her nerves danced in trepidation. She fell to her knees. *Lord God, You see our need. I'm short on the payment. Mr. Johnson is likely a decent man but he's still a businessman. Help him see my intentions are good and honorable. Help him be open to allowing me more time.* She remained on her knees several minutes until she felt calmer. God was just and righteous. He would tend to her needs.

Pushing back little tremors of doubt and nervousness, Madge marched down the stairs. "Mother, I'm on my way to town to take care of things."

Mother nodded. She knew the mortgage was due today, though Madge had spared her the truth and let her assume Madge had earned enough for the payment. She shot a look at Justin and Louisa in the living room bent over a book, too engrossed in each other to even notice her. Resentment tore at her throat. The money she needed had gone to advertise for Justin. So Louisa could be amused.

She choked back her...it wasn't jealousy. She wouldn't admit it. But she'd conveniently forgotten the other unexpected expenses that had sucked at the coins in the can. Momentarily, she closed her eyes. She was only overwrought because of her worries. She would trust God. He was sufficient.

She slipped outside without a backward look. Thankfully the vehicle started on the first try, saving her from having to crawl under the hood.

A few minutes later she parked in front of the bank, pulled on her gloves, took a deep breath and climbed the stone steps. The big doors creaked as she pushed them open. The interior had always seemed to be almost funereal, every sound subdued, the lighting muted, the atmosphere somber.

Madge had come on honest business. She had no reason to shiver. She sucked in the stale air and straightened her shoulders before she approached the teller. Mr. August, a thin, bespectacled man, was a deacon at the church. The way he squinted through his glasses always made her feel as if he examined her under a magnifying glass.

"Mr. August, I'd like to speak to Mr. Johnson, if I may." Her voice came out strong and clear, revealing none of her nervousness.

Mr. August tipped his head up and down as if trying to bring her into focus. Then he nodded. "I'll see if he's available." He shuffled into the far room, the banker's sanctum. No one ventured into the room without being invited. Madge had been there only once before—with Mother, when they'd informed him they wanted to sell the farmland but keep the house. Mr. Johnson had been most agreeable about conducting the business that left them with a mortgaged house but unencumbered by the debt on the land. Madge wasn't unaware the deal had turned out nicely for Mr. Johnson. He had sold the land to a newcomer just before the crash. She supposed the new owner owed money to the banker, too. The crops wouldn't produce enough for feed and seed for the farmer, let alone earn enough for a mortgage payment.

She pressed her lips together. She would not lose her house to a bank that already owned half the town, due to the misfortunes of those who had to cope with the financial difficulties of the day.

Mr. August returned. "He'll see you shortly. Just wait over there." He jabbed his finger toward the three chairs parked against one wall.

Madge sat and waited. She and Mother had done the same last time. No doubt this was part of the way bankers dealt with customers, as if needing to prove they were in control. Her resolve mounted. He might control the money but not her fight. And she would fight to keep the house.

Finally she was called and shepherded into the

office with enough pomp and respect, she might have expected to be presented to King George.

Mr. Johnson half rose and indicated the chair across from his very wide desk. He waited until Madge seated herself and adjusted her hands in her lap.

"How may I help you?"

"I've brought the mortgage payment." She dug the heavy envelope from her purse and handed it to Mr. Johnson.

His lips curled as if the package was noxious, and he put it on the edge of the desk as far from him as possible. "You could have given this to one of the tellers to count."

She nodded. "I realize that, but there is a small problem." *Please, God. Help him agree.* "I'm a bit short."

The way he blinked and drew himself tall, she knew he wasn't seeing this as a small thing.

"I'll pay the full amount. But I need a little more time."

"Where do you propose to get the money? Everyone in the country is in the same position."

"I have some paying customers. I'll find more. You know I'm honest."

He didn't answer. After a long pause, he sighed.

She wished she could let out her breath, too, but

her future—and the future of her mother and sisters—hung on what he decided.

"Here's what I'll do."

Her heart ticked with fear and dread. He opened a drawer and rattled through the contents. If he didn't soon tell her his plan, she was going to pass out from nerves.

"I've let out the Sterling house to some shirt-tail relative of my wife's." He palmed a pair of keys and considered them. "I keep getting possession of houses I can't sell. Neither can I rent them. No one can afford to pay. It's a losing business."

Madge couldn't find it in her heart to feel sorry for his predicament.

"I guess I have to be content with having someone occupy a house and keep up with repairs. Anyway, this nephew of a nephew, or whoever he is, is a bachelor. He's asked me to find someone to clean the house and prepare it for occupancy. Could be, with hard work, you might earn enough to pay what you owe me. His name is George Gratton. He's arriving sometime in the next week or ten days." He handed her the keys. "Can you manage to have the house ready in time?"

"Certainly." If she had to work day and night she would do this job and earn the money to take care of the remainder of the mortgage payment.

She rose and held out her gloved hand. "Thank you, sir. You won't be sorry."

Mr. Johnson's handshake was perfunctory. He already had his attention on the papers before him.

Madge didn't care. She practically skipped from the bank and out to her car. *Thank You, Lord. Forgive my doubts and fears.* She would have to hurry through the work she already had. But if she got done before supper, she'd be able to work at the house in the evening...after she'd taken care of the cow and calf and delivered laundry.

How much should she tell the others? Would they be concerned she'd taken on too much? But it had to be done. Plain and simple, she didn't have any choice. None of them did.

So after supper, she donned her oldest clothes, put buckets and rags in the car and headed for town. No one had expressed any concern when she'd announced her plans. Justin had taken to disappearing after the evening meal. She refused to admit she might have welcomed his company. Only twice more had he gone with her to bring the cow and calf home. She told herself she didn't enjoy his presence more than she should, didn't find his comments amusing, didn't find comfort in being able to talk to him about the farm, the garden and, yes, even feed for the cow.

She'd begin work on the house then visit Joanie, seeing she was nearby. She missed her best friend.

They'd shared secrets and dreams since Madge and her family moved to the area, but lately Madge was too busy to spend time with her. Of course, she couldn't tell Joanie the whole truth of how she felt about Justin, but still, she could enjoy her friend's company, which would cheer her up.

Judd had to force himself to walk away from the farm each evening. He'd discovered how much fun it was to spend a few pleasant hours with Madge after a day of slaving over books with Louisa. Although Louisa enjoyed it a great deal, Judd grew increasingly aware of why he'd abandoned teaching in the first place. He longed for activity, fresh air and open spaces. As he watched Madge work, he itched to help her. Shucks. He ached to do anything physical instead of being the lame, cough-ridden Justin Bellamy.

His only reprieve had been the few hours he'd spent helping Madge. They seemed to find a hundred things to laugh about the few times she'd allowed him to accompany her. He found her an intelligent conversationalist with strong opinions on how the country was being run.

"Run into the ground," she insisted, last time he'd gone with her to bring the calf home.

"And how would you fix things?"

She chuckled. "I don't suppose I could. But it

seems to me there is too much being taken from the poor only to benefit the rich. And shepherding all those single men into camps…why, that's just wrong."

"Some of them are happy enough to have a place to sleep, a meal to eat and work to do."

"I have a friend whose brother is in one of those places. He gets twenty cents a day for backbreaking work. What an insult."

He half agreed but wanted to see her get fired up with passion. "For some, it's better than what they had."

"Pity the man who finds that sort of life a blessing."

He chuckled. "What would you do with them?"

"Treat them with dignity. Don't let the banks take away their land. Do something about the low commodity prices. Seems to me that wouldn't cost the government any more than sending them to camps." She sniffed. "Though from what I hear, the camps aren't costing them much. I don't know how the men will survive winter in the poor quarters." She stopped to stare at him as if he had something to do with the conditions. "Everyone deserves to be treated fairly, honestly and with dignity, don't you think?"

"Yes, ma'am. I certainly do. And let it be known I fully agree with you. That's part of the reason I took this job." He paused to think momentarily of the future. "I'll head back west to the ranching country when the time is right."

She considered him for a long hard moment, searching deep into his thoughts.

He'd done his best to appear open and honest. But there were things he must hide, even though it pained him to do so.

"When will the time be right?"

"I can't say, but I'll know." When he had dealt with the man who stole his mother's savings and robbed her of her home.

"I don't expect you can be a cowboy, though, with your leg and all."

He hadn't thought of that. "More like cook's helper. But, like you said, the fresh air is good for my lungs."

He pulled his thoughts back to the present and reminded himself why he had really taken the job. He set his will firmly to watching for the man, even though it required he give up evening pleasures with Madge. Tired of being crippled, tired of being confined indoors so many hours, after supper he slipped into his comfortable trousers and boots and donned his worn cowboy hat. The soddie was at right angles to the house, and he discovered if he ducked out the door and pressed to the wall until he reached the cover of the barn, he couldn't see the house. He assumed they, likewise, couldn't see him.

Once a safe distance from the farm, he sucked in cleansing air, glad he didn't have to slouch and cough, and he stalked across the prairie with long, hungry strides.

He could have taken his auto, and had several times, but the walk loosened his joints, cleansed his brain and renewed his determination to complete his task.

As usual he tried to be invisible as he headed toward the house where that man would be living. He'd begun to wonder if his information was incorrect. But this evening, his waiting and watching seemed about to be rewarded. Someone had been there. Rugs hung over the railing. The porch had been swept. But the place now looked closed. No lights came from any of the windows, though he viewed it from all four sides just to be certain. He must have missed the man. Perhaps he'd gone for supper or to visit someone. Maybe his newest mark.

He lingered for some time, hoping the object of his interest would return, but as dusk descended he temporarily abandoned his task and turned his footsteps toward home. It was too dark to cross the prairie safely, so he followed the road.

The sound of an automobile reached him, and he jumped into the ditch and hunkered in the shadows.

The car neared. It was Madge. She'd been in town all this time? Had she seen him?

He remained in his position until the car putted away. She often delivered laundry in the evenings but never this late.

He straightened and returned to the road. He'd have to be more careful in the future and somehow find out why she'd been in town so late so he could avoid her.

Discovering the reason for Madge's late outing proved easier than he imagined. The next morning he simply mentioned to Louisa, "Did I see your sister coming in late last night?"

Louisa didn't answer for a moment, then sighed. "I guess she got another job cleaning a house. I wish she didn't have to work so hard, but I'm glad she can."

This must have been the intervention Madge had wanted—a job enabling her to earn enough money to pay the mortgage. "I expect you're grateful she'll manage to keep your home safe."

Louisa lowered her gaze and seemed to consider Mouse, who never left her lap for more than food and time outside. "I'm grateful. Truly, I am."

"Then why do you sound so doubtful?" Could she resent Madge for managing so well? He frequently compared the two girls in his mind. And Sally, who was so quiet and yet always made sure her sisters and mother were taken care of. Madge, though, was the one to note. She had drive and purpose.

"I'm not doubtful. Not really."

He remembered he had asked Louisa a question.

"It's just— I feel guilty that I can't help."

"I'm sure she understands."

"Of course. Though…"

Over the days they had spent studying, Judd had unwittingly learned many of Louisa's secrets and sensed he was about to learn another.

"Sometimes I don't understand," she whispered. "Why must I be content to remain indoors doing practically nothing while Madge does the work of two women?"

Judd laughed. "You call memorizing dates, learning Greek and reading copious amounts nothing? It's hard work in its own way." Yet he wondered as well if life had been fair in giving Madge so much work, though he supposed he meant God rather than life, and he knew he had no right to question his heavenly Father. Nor did Madge seem to mind. She appeared to thrive on hard work.

"It's fun."

"Maybe Madge finds her work fun, too."

Louisa tipped her head. "Are you saying God has made us uniquely suited to our roles in life?"

"I suppose I am." Though it hadn't entered his conscious thoughts. But perhaps God had, likewise, equipped him to do for his mother what his brothers hadn't or wouldn't. When he'd hinted at his plan to Carson, the man had turned all lawyerlike and insisted if a law had been broken, he would have dealt with it.

Where was the justice in that? But because no law had been broken, Carson said there was nothing they could do.

Judd had other ideas.

As Madge hung laundry the next day, she thought of the previous evening. She hadn't been able to get the visit with Joanie she'd hoped for. Not with all Joanie's family hanging about asking questions.

"Who is the young man out at your place?"

"How is your mother?"

"Did you hear the Hendricks up and moved away? I never saw them but heard they had the truck loaded to the gunwales." This from Joanie's father, Mr. Sharp. "Not the first to walk away from his land. 'Spect he won't be the last, either. Times are getting downright tough for everyone."

"Except the bankers who are snapping up the abandoned land and throwing people out of their houses," Madge added.

"Yup. But owning worthless houses no one wants isn't terribly profitable, I'd venture to say."

Madge remembered Mr. Johnson saying something similar. But it elicited no pity in her heart. "Then why don't they just let the people stay?"

Mr. Sharp shrugged. "'Spect it goes against their nature. Bankers are a different breed. I thank the good Lord my business is paid for lock, stock and barrel." Mr. Sharp owned the general store. She knew from her own experience much of the trade was by the barter system. In exchange for necessary supplies, she'd promised part of her butchering when the time came.

Madge noticed the glance Joanie and her mother exchanged. She intended to ask Joanie what they worried about first chance she got.

When she prepared to leave, Joanie pulled her aside. "I'm so glad to see you. It's been ages. But this was an unsatisfactory visit. Let's meet somewhere soon."

Madge agreed. "But I don't know when we can arrange something. I'm cleaning the Sterling house. I'll be busy there every evening for a while."

"Perfect. I'll come and keep you company."

The next night, Madge had barely arrived at the Sterling home before Joanie came skipping down the lane. Madge grinned at her friend and handed her a mop and bucket. "I don't expect you to work, but you can carry this in for me."

"I don't mind helping. It's just so nice to have a

chance to visit." Joanie sounded cheery. Perhaps a bit too much, as if she didn't want to reveal a worry. But Madge knew her friend. The worry could be real or so small it hardly mattered, but Joanie would soon enough share it and end up laughing before she finished relaying her tale of woe.

Madge had done some basic preparation in the front room—hauled out the carpets ready to beat and crowded the furniture into the hallway. Now she and Joanie started a fire in the stove, heated water and tackled a major scrubbing. They visited as they worked.

"Tell me about Louisa's tutor. What did you say his name was?"

"Justin Bellamy, he says."

Joanie giggled. "Do I get the feeling you don't believe him? Why would a man lie about such a simple thing?"

"Maybe not his name but—" She told Joanie about running into a man earlier in town. "I'm certain it's the same man, but Justin isn't anything like him."

"Oh. A mystery. Maybe he's a wanted man." Joanie intended to sound teasing and mysterious.

Madge paused to look out the window. "Wanted? Maybe. But not by the law. I don't see him as that kind of person." But she could see him wanted by a woman. Maybe he was hiding from a soured relationship. Why did the thought both sting and cheer her? It really didn't make any difference, except she needed to know Louisa wasn't getting into something messy. She'd seen the growing fondness in her sister's eyes. Mother must be very happy.

Madge should be, too.

But she couldn't shed her little suspicions about Justin. Nor could she quite dismiss a fledgling jealousy she loathed.

Joanie edged around to plant herself in front of Madge. She grabbed Madge's chin and stared hard at her.

There was no point in avoiding her gaze. Joanie could be quite persistent, so she tried to look mysterious.

Joanie chortled. "You like this man. I can see it in your eyes."

Not even to her best friend would she confess such a thing. Any more than she would tell her why Mother had hired Justin. Not simply to tutor Louisa, but for something far more lasting, if Mother's plans worked out. Madge had no intention of interfering with those plans. "He's not my sort."

"Don't try and pull the wool over my eyes. I've known you far too long."

Madge returned to scrubbing walls and hoped Joanie would do the same or at least drop the subject.

But she didn't. "I remember our little secrets. I

know you want to get married and have a family of your own some day."

"That was before Father died and the country fell into a depression. Who has time to think about such things now?"

"I do." At the sad note in Joanie's voice, Madge forgot scrubbing the walls and turned to her friend.

"Your time will come. Some day."

"I don't see how. Seems all the single men have disappeared. Those still around are needed by their families."

"You mean Connie?"

"His name is Conrad. But he's not the only one."

"Joanie, things will work out."

"How can you be sure? People often have to live with disappointment." She squeezed the water out of a rag and returned to scrubbing.

Madge did the same, but she wasn't prepared to leave the subject just yet. "God provides. Like this job for me. I need more money for the mortgage. I prayed. And even though I didn't trust God wholly, He answered."

"Here I am worried about not having a boyfriend while you struggle to keep your house. I'm sorry."

Madge again heard a note of worry. She faced her friend. "What else is bothering you?"

"I guess we're all in the same boat. Father gets lots of goods for trade, but that doesn't pay the bills."

Guilt struck Madge, and she vowed to buy no more than absolutely necessary unless she could pay cash. Right now that meant she'd buy nothing. Every penny she made would go to the banker. "I wish things would turn around soon. In the meantime, what can we do but the best we can?"

"I know, and I don't mean to complain."

They worked in silence for a bit.

Madge's thoughts went to Justin. It was only reasonable he had his own interests to pursue in the evenings, but despite her vow to pretend she didn't care, she half hoped he'd join her when she went to get the cow. Nor would she object to his company while she cleaned this house. Not that she didn't appreciate Joanie's presence.

"Hello? Are you there?"

She realized Joanie stared at her, amusement drawing her eyes upward.

"I was concentrating."

"Lost in a dream world. Didn't even hear my question."

"Sorry. What?"

"He must be quite the charmer."

"Who?" As if she didn't know. Her cheeks burned with guilty heat.

"Ho, ho. So if it isn't Justin, than who?" Joanie ceased work to squint and consider. "Nope. Can't think of anyone but Justin who might make you get all flustered."

"I am not flustered." Madge determinedly asked after mutual friends. When had Joanie seen them, and how were they? From the look on her friend's face, she knew Joanie understood her intention and played along out of the goodness of her heart.

They finished the room. "It's a bigger job than I thought it would be," Madge said as she stretched her back to ease an ache between her shoulders. "I'm not sure when this man—George Gratton—is coming." Nor how much he was paying. Hopefully more than twenty cents a day.

"What do you know about Mr. Gratton?"

"Not a thing, except he's some distant relative of Mrs. Johnson's and is unmarried."

Joanie frowned. "How is it that you get two un-married men in your life and I get none?"

Madge laughed, not fooled by her friend's pretend annoyance. "You've had eyes for no one but Connie since you were fourteen years old and he fell out of the tree into your lap. I think you secretly branded him right then and there."

"Conrad. And I did not. Besides, what difference does it make? He has his family to care for."

"Things will work out."

Joanie tossed her head. "So you say. Sometimes I

think you simply refuse to admit anything you can't control."

The words stung. "I do not."

"Sure you do. How often have you pretended you didn't want something if you knew you couldn't have it? Like the time Louisa got the dress fabric you wanted. All of a sudden you didn't care."

"That was five years ago. I was still a child. I hope I've outgrown being jealous of my sister."

"Have you?"

She wished she could assure her friend she had. She didn't like the little resentment burning a hole in her heart that it was Louisa who had Justin by her side all day, his attention focused on her. "He's not my sort." As soon as the words were out, she knew she had given away her secret.

But Joanie didn't laugh or tease. "Things will work out. Didn't you just say so?"

Madge refused to answer. It was one thing to ask God to help her when she needed something good and noble and right. When it was selfish and involved hurting her sister, she had no right to ask.

Joanie chuckled. "What a pair of worrying old maids we've become." Only her eyes didn't laugh.

Madge knew why. Could they both end up alone for the rest of their lives? It was a dreadful thought, but a real possibility.

She would not think of Justin Bellamy. Even if

he proved to be noble and honest and all the things she admired in a man because, whether he knew it or not, he would belong to Louisa.

God, help me not to be a jealous sister.

But even prayer did not erase the forbidden longing.

Chapter Five

Judd watched the house as Madge and her friend cleaned. So this was the job she'd gotten. He leaned back in the shadows, fighting anger and a protectiveness that curled his fists. Surely George wasn't making Madge his next mark. But no, that didn't make sense. Madge didn't have anything to give the man. Did she? He carefully reviewed everything she'd told him, things Louisa had said, even things he'd overheard in conversations among the women. Nothing indicated they had anything but debt.

The girls in the house laughed as they worked. He grinned, finding enjoyment in seeing Madge having fun.

A long, silent ache slid down his throat and wrapped around his heart. He wished he could join them. If only he didn't have to hide the truth about who he was and what he intended.

His insides boiled with nameless yearning. He must deal with his restlessness before it boiled over and he did something he'd regret. Like storm into the house and demand to know why she was aiding his foe. Not that she knew.

A deeper truth couldn't be ignored. He wanted to push inside and confess everything. He ached to be honest with Madge.

Glad he'd shed the Justin Bellamy disguise, he turned on his heel and strode down the back lane, thankful for the shadows to hide him. His gait ate up block after block until he reached the edge of town. He stood and stared out at the prairie, dotted here and there with dark shapes of houses, little fireflies of lights coming on in scattered windows. He sucked in air until his edginess settled. Then he examined his feelings.

He hated being dishonest with Madge. He wanted to tell her every fear and anger and frustration he felt. Yet what choice did he have but to continue his deception?

Slowly, a cunning idea grew. Perhaps this was for the best. Madge had access to the comings and goings of George Gratton. Judd could use the information to his advantage.

For several minutes, he warred with himself. How could he think he cared for Madge yet be prepared to use her as an unknowing spy? But surely she'd understand if she found out. After all, she was a fighter, prepared to do what she had to to keep a roof over their heads. Yet he knew her stubborn struggle to keep her family safe wasn't the same as his quest.

However, he hoped she would never discover his duplicity until he saw the man punished—see justice carried out—for what he'd done to Judd's mother.

He'd tell Madge the truth when the time was right.

His mind set on a course; his jaw tight, his insides tense, he strode back into town.

It felt good to stretch his legs. He concentrated on the way his muscles released pent-up energy to avoid the guilt jabbing at his thoughts.

The house was again in front of him. He stopped to stare. Too late, he realized Madge had come to the lane to empty her bucket and had likely watched him for several seconds.

"Why, if it isn't Justin Bellamy, his limp all gone. And what, Mr. Bellamy, brought about this sudden healing?"

Caught. All because he had been carrying on a little battle with himself. He had no choice but to explain—but how honest must he be?

Madge hadn't believed him from the beginning. Anything he said now would be met with double doubts.

Even in the low evening light, her gaze was direct, demanding.

He couldn't tell the whole truth. "You're right. I am the man you ran into that day."

"I knew it. Why the pretense?"

"I have to hide my true identity."

"Have to?" Her tone was hard.

"Let me explain."

"Oh, please do. I'm dying to hear your story."

Yes, she was going to find it hard to accept any explanation he gave. "Justin Bellamy isn't my real name." He sorely wanted her to know him as Judd, but how much dare he risk?

"Do you intend to tell me who you really are?"

"First, I must have your promise not to tell anyone my true name."

She busied herself with the mop and bucket before she answered. "How can I promise when I don't know the reason?"

Ah. He understood her concern. Should he be a culprit, she'd feel honor bound to turn him over to the law. But how could she consider it possible of him? "Madge." He spoke softly. "Do you think I would have a dishonest reason for doing this?"

She chuckled—more a regretful than merry sound. "You're asking me to trust your honesty when you just admitted you're living a lie?"

"I'll try to explain, but surely you know I wouldn't be doing something morally or legally wrong." It stung that she would doubt him, but what could he expect? He had deceived her. He would tell her his story and hope it made her more forgiving. "I told you my mother lost her savings."

"Not unlike many people."

"No. Only she lost hers to a con man."

She nodded, still unbelieving but waiting for more.

"He pretended to love her to gain her confidence. He promised he'd marry her. She believed him. When he said he had an investment opportunity that would double her money, she believed that, too. Only once he got his hands on the funds, he disappeared. It almost destroyed my mother. Cost her her house and savings."

Still Madge waited, though as she faced the house, he believed he saw a flicker of sympathy in her eyes. Perhaps it'd only been a flare from the light coming from inside, because when she turned back to him, her expression was hard. "I'm sorry, but I fail to see what this has to do with me or my family."

"I searched for him for several months. Learned he—" If he said the man was about to move into the community, she would no doubt put the facts together with her task of cleaning this house. He didn't want her alerted. "I learned he had moved into this community to play his con game again."

Madge studied him. "Most men are moving out of the area."

"Must be a few moving in."

Reluctantly she nodded. "I guess."

"I aim to find him and stop him from doing to another woman what he did to my mother."

Her expression revealed a struggle with doubt and sympathy.

He caught her shoulder and looked hard into her dark, steady eyes. "If he hears my name, he'll figure out who I am. How long do you think it will take him to guess why I'm here? Warned, he'll likely move on but perhaps with someone's savings in his pocket."

She held his gaze, steady, demanding and something more—something that caught at his heart and tugged it gently in her direction.

"What's your name?" Her low question almost broke through the barriers he must keep firmly in place. He forced resolve into his thoughts.

"You vow you won't tell anyone?"

She nodded, her look full of so much promise he struggled to find his voice.

"Judd. Judd Kirk."

"Judd." His name on her lips was sweet as a kiss.

He looked deep into her eyes, his world shifting to higher, rarer air.

"You haven't found the man yet?" Her words sent his thoughts back to his plan.

"No, but I'm close."

She nodded, not releasing her dark-eyed hold on him for even a heartbeat. "And when you do?"

"I'll make him pay." He'd force the man to give back the funds. He'd somehow make him suffer as much as his mother had. But if he hadn't been so trapped by Madge's intensity, he might have guarded his words more carefully. He wished he had when her expression hardened.

"You're talking revenge."

"No. I'm talking justice."

"What about the law?"

"There's nothing they can do."

She considered him a moment. "But isn't God the righteous judge?"

Her words were soft but challenging, striking at a place between his faith and his life that held nothing of substance, only waiting silence. His sole defense was to point out things widening the breach. "Can you look around at how this world is going and say God is treating us fairly? Why doesn't He do something to stop this drought and everything else tearing this country apart?"

She shook her head back and forth. "I don't know why bad things happen, but I believe we can trust God to take care of us."

"Could you say that if you lost your house?"

She grew fierce. "I'm not going to let that happen."

Fierceness grew in his heart, too, and edged his words. "My mother didn't expect to lose hers, either. She trusted a man. I intend to see her get some recompense." Hoping to make his actions more acceptable, he added, "And make sure that man doesn't repeat his game." He hadn't realized until this conversation how much he wanted more than justice. He'd always soothed his conscience by telling himself he only wanted to stop the man from cheating another woman.

"Judgment is in God's hands. If you are determined to exact vengeance, you will surely be twice bitten."

He crossed his arms over his chest. "I don't know what you mean." Wasn't sure he wanted to. He would make that man pay for stealing his mother's house and savings. Nothing she said would change his mind.

"Not only are you stricken with bitterness at what happened to your mother, but if you take things into your own hands you will be touched by the evil of vengeance." She moved closer, rested her warm hand on his forearm.

The touch seared his nerves, stung his thoughts and made him waver. But God's justice took too long. His mother shouldn't have to wait until eternity to see it.

"Judd. I like that name. Suits you so much better than Justin."

He covered her hand with his. "I like it better, too." Especially the way she said it.

"Judd, I don't want to see you hurt by taking on the role of avenger."

Caught in her steady gaze, he couldn't argue.

But he couldn't agree, either.

"I'll not do anything wrong."

She lowered her eyes, leaving him floundering for determination about his course of action.

"I pray you will learn that God's way is best."

He squeezed her fingers. "I appreciate your concern."

Neither of them moved. She kept her head down. He let himself explore the feel of her hand beneath his—strong from hard work and yet soft. Just like Madge herself.

She sighed. "I've been trying to guess who this man you want to find is, but I can't think of anyone. It would be awful if it was someone I know."

"Not too likely. He's only an obscure relative of one of the families." He hoped she wouldn't take that bit of information any further. "I don't expect he's making himself too visible." Entirely true at this point. "Now enough of this. Can I help with anything?"

Slowly she eased her hand away and grabbed the

mop and bucket. "I'm done for the day. Mr. Johnson left a note on the door saying the occupant would be here in two days' time. I'll have everything ready by then. Mrs. Johnson sent over a stack of bedding, so I'm to make up the beds. Though I have no idea if I should make them all or—" She shrugged.

Judd followed her to the house and scooped up the rest of her cleaning supplies. "Mind if I catch a ride back home with you? I walked to town."

"Leg doesn't hurt much now?" He heard the teasing tone in her voice.

"Not when I'm Judd Kirk. Though I did hurt my leg just as I told you."

"I expect your cough is better when you're Judd Kirk, too."

Ah, would he ever hear his name from her mouth without it strumming his heart like a harp? "Lots better, thank you."

She grinned at him and they both laughed.

Judd. She liked the name. Just as she'd liked the cowboy she'd bumped into weeks ago. Since that day, she'd allowed her fancy to build a solid picture of him in her imagination. She'd envisioned long, thrilling rides clinging to his waist as a black horse galloped across the land. She'd ignored her suspicions that Justin and Judd—the name sang through her brain—might well be the same person. Instead, she'd given him a double. Now her foolish, childish pretendings had taken form and substance.

She shifted and gripped the steering wheel as they headed toward home. His presence filled far more of the space beside Madge than the bulk of his body.

His plans for revenge crowded her thoughts, and as she focused on what he'd said, she was able to push her embarrassment and discomfort to the back of her mind. She had never considered getting revenge on anyone, but somehow she suspected it truly had a scorpion tail of regret. She must convince him his chosen course of action might destroy him.

For Louisa's sake, of course. She didn't want to see her sister dealing with the aftermath.

She shuddered as she thought how, if he persisted, Judd could be hurt, or get himself into trouble with the law.

"I know it's not my business, but I really think there must be another way to deal with this man you mention without stooping to revenge."

Judd chuckled. "I'll not do anything illegal or sinful, if that's what worries you." He sounded mighty pleased at her concern.

"I just don't want my family, Louisa especially, involved, even by association, with something that could bring hurt or harm." There, she'd said it rather well. No reason for him to read more than normal caution in her words.

"I fail to see how what I do will in any way affect your family. And why Louisa especially?"

Because Mother plans for Louisa to become your wife. But she could hardly tell him the truth any more than she would allow herself to acknowledge how the thought stung. "I suppose I'm being overly cautious, but we've all done what we can to protect Louisa. Her health has always been a bit delicate."

"She doesn't strike me as particularly frail."

Did she detect a note of impatience in his voice? But no, she'd observed them together often enough to know he treated Louisa with nothing but patience and gentleness. It would be wise to change the topic of conversation before she revealed more than she should. "You're not really planning to go back to the ranch as cook's helper, are you?"

His laughter rang out, filled the small space and raced through her heart like fresh water in a summer-drenched stream.

She gritted her teeth. It was going to be hard to remember Louisa's claim on this man. *God, give me grace. Help me be concerned only with protecting Louisa and helping Judd.*

The next evening, Judd helped her carry the clean laundry to the automobile and climbed in beside her. "I'll ride along with you and help with the deliveries."

"You're still Justin." He hunched inside the baggy clothes of his tutor role. She longed to see him in his jeans and the cotton shirt that fit across his shoulders, allowing her to admire his strength.

"I must keep my secret from your sisters and mother."

"I still think you're wrong." She'd thought of little else all day, praying for wisdom to say something to make him change his mind. "It says in the Bible that vengeance belongs to God alone, who will recompense."

He drew in air until she wondered if his lungs would explode. "I can see this is going to be a problem for you. So let's deal with it and be done. I told you I won't do anything wrong, so can we stop calling it revenge? I only want to see justice done."

Justice and revenge were too closely related for Madge's peace of mind, but she didn't want to spend their few precious hours together arguing. "Fine. I'll let it go."

"Great."

"So what else should we talk about?"

He chuckled. "I'm dying to know what you were like as a little girl."

"A bit of a tomboy, I suppose. I liked to follow my father around and help him. I must have been a dreadful nuisance, but he never seemed to mind. When Mother objected I was not as ladylike as she wished, Father always said, 'Leave her be. You never know when it might come in handy to know how to do these things.'"

"Seems he was right." He shifted so he could see her face.

She darted a look at him, saw his gentle smile, sucked in a sharp breath and jerked her attention back to the road, trying to ignore how his look made her feel—not that she could even find a word to describe it. Special. That was the closest she came. His smile made her feel special.

"You manage very well. I've admired you as you work so hard. Fact is, many times I've had to remind myself I'm Justin, a teacher, not as strong as I want to be, when all the time I've wanted to be Judd and haul those heavy baskets up the stairs for you."

Her gaze edged sideways. Her heart beat a frenzied rhythm against her ribs as she stared into his dark intensity. His smile filled his eyes.

"You did?" Oh, but her voice sounded squeaky and surprised.

"Sure did." He reached out, caught a strand of hair trailing across her cheek and pushed it into place. "You work too hard."

The car had drifted almost to a standstill. She tore her gaze from his and back to the road, trying to assess his words. Did he care about her? Her heart sang a secret song, but she stilled it. He was not for her. Mother had picked him for Louisa.

Or had she? She'd picked Justin Bellamy for Louisa. There was no such person. Judd Kirk was a strong cowboy. An outdoor man. A—

She slammed the door on her thoughts. She would not look for excuses. God saw her inner being. No amount of mental wrangling would make her envy pleasing to Him.

They reached town. He insisted on carrying the baskets of laundry to the door for her, limping up the path at her side.

"Others need to believe I'm Justin Bellamy. I can't afford to let that man guess my real identity," he said when she mentioned it.

She wanted to protest further but feared it would bring a wedge between them, so she let it go. For now.

After she'd collected the next day's work from her various customers, she headed for the Sterling house. Judd helped her carry in supplies. "I need to scout around. I'll be back in—what? An hour? Two?"

"Better make it two. I want to have everything ready tonight. Mr. Gratton arrives tomorrow."

"Two hours, then." He touched the brim of his hat.

She hated watching him leave and wanted to say something more about his intention, but she only nodded, then headed indoors.

* * *

Judd strode away as if his mission required it, but George Gratton was the man he sought. He had no reason to look further. He simply had to observe the man and wait for the right time and situation.

Madge's convictions about revenge had seared his conscience. But he could not walk away from his goal. Mr. Gratton must be stopped. Justice must be served.

Madge did not know she worked in the house of his enemy, and he didn't intend to tell her.

He had two hours to pass and nothing to do. He wandered to the edge of town and stared out across the prairie. A man could settle down here and be content. Why had he thought he wanted to go back to the foothills and ranching? The idea no longer fit. A bit of land of his own, a nice little house, a wife—

A chuckle sprang to his lips. His land and house were just wisps in his mind but "wife" had shape and form. Madge. He reflected on the idea. She'd make a very nice wife—hardworking, cheerful, determined.

Buoyed by thoughts of Madge, he moseyed back to the center of town and parked on a bench outside the store to wait. He listened to conversations around him, hoping to hear something about George Gratton.

A man sauntered by and paused to study Judd. "You waiting for something?"

Judd explained he was tutor to Miss Louisa. "Her sister is cleaning the Sterling house."

"I heard someone was moving in."

Judd risked asking more. "Anyone you know?"

"Heard it was a relative of the banker's wife."

Judd already knew that. He wanted to know why. "What do you suppose brought him here?"

The man leaned on the wall and picked his teeth with a straw. "Heard he was going to work at the bank. Suppose he'll be helping the banker take people's homes from them." He chomped down on the straw and then spat it out.

Judd expected Mr. Gratton's methods would serve the banker well. He could see how Gratton could use this to his advantage, too. With access to personal financial information, he'd learn who he should befriend. His situation would enable him to steal from someone else. Judd clenched down on his back teeth. He would see that another helpless woman or vulnerable family wasn't hurt by this man.

Two hours later he returned to the house. Madge stowed cleaning supplies in the car and looked up at his approach.

"Any success?"

He drew back, at a loss over her question.

"Locating this man you seek?"

"Oh. Yes. I'm certain I've located him."

She quirked an eyebrow and waited. When he

didn't offer any more information, she prodded. "Someone I know?"

"Can't say. Doesn't matter. I'll watch him and when the time is right—" He pressed his lips into a grimace.

She edged closer and touched his arm. "Judd, please reconsider. I fear there is a fine line between justice and anger."

She cared. The knowledge almost made him willing to give up his plan. Almost. But he couldn't shake the burden of guilt pressing against his heart. "If I'd been home, I would have stopped him before he stole Mother's money. Now the best I can do is—"

"Can you get her money back?"

"Maybe."

"Can you get her house back?"

"Depends on whether the bank has sold it already." Mother said she didn't care about the house, but Judd was certain she only wanted her sons to feel better.

"Have you prayed about this?"

Her words tore at his conscience, warring with his faith. But he didn't see how he could trust God to fix this problem.

He hadn't told Mother his plans. He'd guessed her reaction would be much like Madge's. "This is something I have to do."

They got into the automobile, but if Judd thought

Madge had forgotten the subject, she proved him wrong.

"Judd, you can't undo the past. Even if you feel you failed your mother by not being there, this is not going to change anything."

"I did fail her. As the oldest, I should have protected her."

"What about Carson? He's a lawyer. Why didn't he stop the man?"

He'd posed the same question to his brother. Carson had insisted Mother had not told anyone her plans, had not consulted anyone. None of them had known what she'd done until she'd informed them she would be moving out of the house. Only after much prodding had Carson managed to squeeze the truth from her.

"I intend to stop the man."

Madge made a sound of distress. "I fear for you."

"You do?" The idea tasted like honey. She had both hands on the steering wheel, and he reached over and squeezed one. "I'm glad you care."

A jolt ran through her arm to his. "Of course I do. My family could be hurt by anything you do."

He removed his hand and stared out the window. He didn't want her to care for her family's sake. He wanted her to care for his sake. Though either way, it would make no difference. He had his mind set on this course. The man had to pay, had to be stopped. Judd must somehow make up for failing his mother.

Chapter Six

Madge dropped Justin at the soddie, refusing his help to unload the baskets of laundry. She needed the time to sort out her feelings before she went indoors.

Judd had accused her of caring. She hadn't denied it. She couldn't. But the knowledge left her shaken and struggling for mental balance. Her only defense was the argument she'd given him—what he did had the potential to impact her family, especially Louisa.

Louisa had not yet gone to her room when Madge entered the house. She sat in an upright chair, Mouse in her lap.

Madge stiffened her spine, knowing something was amiss. "You should be in bed by now. You'll overtire yourself with all this studying and staying up late."

Louisa gently stroked Mouse, then lifted her head

and gave Madge a look fit to cause her heart to stall. "Mother told me about Justin."

Madge quirked an eyebrow. "I'm sorry. Is that supposed to mean something?"

"She didn't hire him just to be my tutor. She picked him as my future husband."

Madge sat down.

"She said you knew."

Madge could do no more than nod. In a secret corner of her thoughts, she'd clutched the idea that neither Judd nor Louisa knew of Mother's plan, so she wasn't really stealing from her sister. Now she could no longer deceive herself. She resisted an urge to say she'd seen him first.

"And yet you spend every evening in his company." Louisa's voice rang with accusation. It was an exaggeration. They'd spent only a few evenings together.

"You have him all day. Besides, I don't invite him along. He has business in town so he finds it convenient to catch a ride."

"He has his own auto which, I'm sure I don't need to point out, is in much better shape than ours. Besides, what's this business he has?"

Madge tried to ignore the little surge of pleasure that she knew Judd's secret and Louisa did not. A flood of guilt followed—hard. How petty to feel in competition with her sister. "Ask him yourself. After all, you two should be getting to know one another better."

They smiled at each other, but Madge wasn't fooled. Behind Louisa's smile lay a scowl, just as one lay behind her own.

"I'm tired. I'm going to bed. Do you want help?"

"No, thank you."

Good, because I don't feel like helping you.

But a few minutes later, in her room, her uncharitable attitude haunted her. *Lord, forgive me. I've known from the beginning what Mother's plans were. I knew better than to think about Judd in a romantic way.* She had no one to blame but herself that her heart had betrayed her. She'd let her imagination take her so far off course.

Holding her Bible on her lap, she bowed over it and prayed for wisdom to deal with this situation and strength to do what was right. Paying no attention to where her bookmark lay, she let the pages fall open and skimmed over the words before her. She'd marked the last two verses of a psalm. "Search me, O God, and know my heart; try me, and know my thoughts; and see if there be any wicked way in me, and lead me in the way everlasting."

Oh God, give me the strength to keep my face toward what is right. Judd cannot belong to me. Not without hurting Louisa, and I couldn't live with myself if I stole him from her.

Even as she murmured the words, she wondered if Judd might have something to say about the arrangement. No. She would not keep allowing herself excuses and loopholes.

Judd had accompanied them to church each Sunday. Today was no different. The five of them crowded into the car. Judd offered to drive, so Madge made sure Louisa sat beside him. She crawled in the back with Mother and Sally and pretended she didn't see his look of surprise.

When they got to church she lingered behind, waiting for Judd to follow the family into a pew. He hesitated, glancing at her. She smiled and nodded as if everything was fine when, inside, sharp talons scraped at her heart. Why must he be all she'd ever dreamed of in a man? Not as Justin, but as Judd. Strong, adventuresome, determined—her eyes stung with worry. Though he'd said nothing about how he planned to make the man he sought pay, she feared his determination would end in disaster.

He waited a moment, and when she made no move toward joining the family, he sat—but not before she'd seen his mouth draw down in resignation.

She spotted Joanie and went to sit with her.

Pastor Jones had a good sermon. At least she suspected he did because of the way others in the congregation nodded agreement and murmured,

"Amen." She couldn't concentrate, as her gaze insisted on sliding toward Judd, sitting calmly beside Louisa. Anyone watching would think he listened intently. She wondered if he did. From the little she heard of the sermon, she understood the pastor exhorted them to trust God in these hard times.

"He is the answer to our suffering and sorrow. He is the One who offers hope, justice and everything we need for godliness and contentment."

Throughout the service, Joanie shifted and glanced around. Something bothered her.

As soon as the final "Amen" had been said and people began to move about, Joanie turned to her. "Conrad isn't here. None of his family is. Something's wrong. I know it."

It was unusual, but perhaps not a cause for worry.

"I'm going out to see for myself."

"How will you get there?" The Burnses' farm was ten miles from town, and Joanie's family didn't own a car. Nor even a horse and buggy.

"Can you take me?"

"Certainly." She welcomed the chance to do something away from home, away from Judd and Louisa and the knowledge of her forbidden attraction. "I'll take the others home first."

"Hurry. I'm terribly worried."

Madge squeezed Joanie's arm. "You're disappointed because you hoped to see him."

Joanie's eyes crinkled in amusement and embarrassment. "True. But then, it's not as if I see him any other time."

Madge gathered up her family and hurried them to the car, explaining she'd promised to take Joanie to the Burnses'. "She's worried because none of them showed up today."

Mother tsked. "I do hope they aren't sick."

"They should give up and move on," Louisa said.

Sally gasped. "Louisa, how can you suggest such a thing? What will they have if they leave?"

Louisa sighed. "Surely there are better places with more opportunity. I can't think it's as bad all over the country as right here."

Madge kept her opinion to herself. From what she'd heard, people were worse off in many other places. "Hurry up, girls. Joanie is waiting for me."

"Where's Justin?" Louisa demanded. "We can't leave him behind."

The thought crossed Madge's mind to do exactly that. She knew he often walked to town in the dusk. But the others only knew him as Justin, with a bum leg and poor lungs.

"There he is." Louisa waved, indicating they were ready to leave.

Justin limped over and crawled in the passenger side. That left Madge to drive and share the front seat with him.

She didn't care. She ignored him for the few minutes required to reach home. But it took a great deal of effort to concentrate on the conversation in the back and on her driving.

The trip seemed longer than usual. She put it down to her need to hurry for Joanie's sake—not her acute awareness of Judd so close, nor his probing glances. If they'd been alone, he would have surely demanded an explanation for her strange behavior. He couldn't miss the fact she'd gone out of her way to avoid him. Thankfully Mother and her two sisters shared the car, preventing him from making a comment.

She pulled up to the house and waited for everyone to get out. Mother and her sisters hurried inside. Judd gave no indication he meant to get out.

"Any objection to me going along?"

She wanted to argue, but try as she might, she couldn't dredge up a single word of protest.

"I'll switch to the back when you pick up your friend."

Still, she could do no more than stare at him.

"Who knows what you'll find at the farm? Might be a wreck and you'll be grateful for my company."

"Fine." As she drove from the yard, she glimpsed Louisa at the window and instantly regretted her decision. But it was too late, and she didn't want to waste the day arguing with him. But then, she also didn't want to confront the questions she expected he wanted to ask. So she began talking about Conrad's family.

"Conrad's father died several years ago. He's the eldest and has been running the place since. He has four younger siblings. Mary is...well, she must be fourteen by now. Then there's Quint—he's a couple years younger than Mary but a big boy. I expect he's a lot of help to Connie now. The two little girls are six and seven. Rosie and Pearl."

"Uh-huh."

"They live on a farm. But you know how farming is right now. The drought, the dust, the grasshoppers." Her voice trailed off. These were all things he was well aware of.

He nodded, his gaze fixed on her as if realizing why she poured out all this information.

She rushed on so he wouldn't get a chance to probe. "Connie's mother has been sick a lot lately. I expect she's under the weather again, and Connie didn't feel like he should leave her to attend church."

"Perhaps we should stop by and ask the doctor to visit."

"Conrad's mother refuses to see the doctor. Says she can't afford to pay. Besides, I don't think it's up to me to make such a decision."

"I suppose not, though I would expect you'd do what you had to do, with or without permission."

He sounded as if he thought doing so was admirable, and she allowed herself a quick glance. And instantly regretted it. His dark gaze filled with questions, demands, regrets....

She swallowed hard and forced her attention back to the road.

A regretful sigh whistled past his teeth. "Just as I'd expect honesty from you if I have somehow upset you."

"Honesty from me?" Her voice squeaked a protest. "Now, that's ironic from a man pretending to be something he isn't."

"You know my reasons, and I've been honest enough with you about them."

"Perhaps because I found you out?"

"Maybe I wanted you to."

At the gentleness in his tone, she couldn't stop herself from glancing at him again. At the teasing smile on his lips, she understood he was trying to correct whatever had made her avoid him so pointedly all day. Thankfully they had reached town, and she was saved from trying to explain.

Joanie stood on the front step waiting. She ran to the car as Judd stepped out. "Oh, excuse me." She ducked to peer at Madge.

"Joanie, this is Justin Bellamy."

"The tutor?" She eyed him up and down, winked

at Madge, then, before Madge could do or say anything, climbed in. "Let's be on our way."

Madge hoped no one would detect any hint of the heat flooding her cheeks. Joanie was wrong. There was no romance. Nothing to make her nudge Madge and giggle as Judd closed the door after her.

"I didn't invite him along," she whispered before Judd climbed into the back.

Joanie took the conversation no further. Instead she amused them with tales of adventures she and Conrad had been on. Madge knew it was her friend's way of keeping her worries at bay. By the time they arrived at the farm, Madge was almost as worried as Joanie. It was unusual for none of them to attend church. Mary often brought the younger children if her mother was ill. And Connie made an effort to come, if only to see his favorite gal—Joanie.

They turned down the trail toward the house. The two little Burns girls sat dejectedly on the step as Madge pulled the car to a halt. The wheels hadn't ceased rolling before Joanie bolted from the car and rushed to them.

"What's wrong? Where is everyone?"

"They's inside with Momma," Rosie said.

"Momma is very sick." Pearl shuddered.

Joanie hugged them both, but her glance sought out the mysteries of the house.

"I'll take care of them," Madge murmured. "You

go see what's going on." She pulled the two trembling girls to her side.

Judd held the door open for Joanie. "Can I help?"

Joanie shivered. "I don't know." She slipped inside.

Madge edged the girls away from the step, into the sunshine. She wanted to ask them how long their momma had been sick, but it was plain as jam on toast that the children were near to breaking down. Instead she sat on the empty water trough and pulled them to her side.

Judd had not followed. She told herself she wasn't disappointed as she watched him walk around the house. A few minutes later, he appeared with two half-grown kittens and handed one to each of the girls. "Found some lonely kitties just begging for attention."

The girls buried their faces in the soft fur and murmured affectionately to their pets.

Madge's eyes stung with appreciation at his gesture. "Thank you," she mouthed.

He nodded and sat by Rosie. As with Madge, the closed door to the house seemed to have an unusual pull on his gaze.

Her heart lifted with relief when Mary came out and stood motionless. Then she saw the girl wasn't motionless at all. Her shoulders shook.

"I'll stay here. You go talk to her," Judd whispered.

She left him with the younger girls and hurried over to pull Mary into a hug. But Mary resisted.

"What's wrong?"

"Momma."

"How is she?"

Mary rocked back and forth and sobbed gently.

Madge did not like the way Mary acted. As if… What should she do? She shot a desperate glance at Judd.

He eased away from the little girls, making sure they remained with their attention on the cats, and came to her side. "What's the matter?"

"I'm not sure."

"Wait here," he said to Mary and, taking Madge's hand, pulled her into the house. She knew the way and led him to Mrs. Burns's bedroom where she lay abed, Conrad at her side, his hair tousled, his eyes shadowed as if he hadn't slept in days.

Joanie pressed to his side, rubbing his shoulder. Tears streaked her face.

Judd stepped forward and touched his fingers to Mrs. Burns's throat. "She's gone."

Conrad nodded. "I know," he choked out.

"How long?" Judd asked.

"This morning. But I couldn't bring myself to admit it. Mary only just realized when Joanie came."

He shuddered, then reached up and claimed one of Joanie's hands.

Judd looked around, then murmured to Madge, "Didn't you say there was a younger boy?"

"Quint."

"Where is he?"

Conrad glanced about, as if only now aware of his brother's absence. "Likely gone to the barn."

Judd stood. "You need to inform the pastor. Let the neighbors know." But no one moved.

"Can you do it?" Joanie murmured.

"Of course." He captured Madge's hand and pulled her from the room with him. "Get Mary doing something. I'll find Quint and send him to the neighbors to ask them to go for the pastor."

She didn't move. The shock of seeing Mrs. Burns lying there dead and cold, of seeing Conrad so shaken, left her stunned.

"Madge, they need our help."

Suddenly her fears and concerns exploded. "How will they manage? Their father is already dead. The girls are so young. Mary only fourteen, and now she'll have to be the mother. I can't even think."

He grabbed her shoulders and turned her to face him.

She clung to his dark gaze, searching for and finding strength, encouragement and something she knew she must deny, but at the moment needed so badly she couldn't move.

"Madge, don't try and solve all their problems at once."

She nodded. And shuddered. She wanted to collapse in his arms and pretend none of the past few minutes were real.

He squeezed her shoulders. She sucked in a strengthening gasp.

"You'll be fine." He seemed to know she was now ready to face the difficult task ahead and dropped his hands from her shoulders before going to find Quint. For two quick breaths she felt rudderless, lost, then she hurried outside and found Mary shivering against the corner of the house. "Let's make tea for everyone." Mary allowed Madge to lead her indoors. Over the girl's shoulder she saw Judd talking to Quint, and then the boy raced across the field to the nearest neighbor. He smiled encouragement as he strode over to join her.

Together they managed to get Mary busy in the kitchen and persuade the little girls to have sandwiches. Joanie drew Conrad from the bedroom and convinced him to eat something.

By then the neighbors had arrived. Quint tried to escape to the barn again, but Judd gently urged him to join the family in the kitchen.

Shortly afterwards the pastor drove in, accompanied by his sweet wife. But the girls clung to Madge, Conrad to Joanie, and Judd looked to Quint, who watched for signals as to what he should do. Just as Madge watched Judd for smiles of encouragement and nods of approval. He seemed to know exactly what to do and took care of a hundred details no one else had the heart to deal with—like the scrawny cow bellowing to be milked and the eggs waiting to be gathered. He filled the water pails from the well and replenished the coal bucket so they could keep the kettle boiling as neighbors continued to arrive and offer help. According to the custom of the area, the body would lie in the house, with neighbors and family keeping constant vigil until the funeral service.

He must have also sent a message to Madge's family, as Sally arrived bearing a chocolate cake. She rushed over to hug Madge. "Are you okay?"

Madge clung to her sister. "I can't stop wondering how they'll survive. The children are much younger than we are, and yet I wonder how we'd manage if Mother left us."

"Pray to God we won't have to find out. Now let's see what needs to be done." She glanced around. "Seems pretty organized already." Surprise filled her voice.

"Judd—Justin got things going."

"Very good." Sally practically rubbed her hands together as she headed for the kitchen to add her help.

Madge stood in the yard watching neighbors slip in and out of the house, clustering in knots to discuss the loss. Then the conversations shifted to other things. It all felt impossible. Like a dream from which she would awaken and thank God it wasn't real. Only it was. It had left her shaken to the core. She looked about. Judd talked to a couple of the men, Quint at his side.

Not giving herself a chance to consider her actions, Madge made her way to him. She longed to press close, feel the comfort of his arms around her. But such comfort did not belong to her. She would allow herself only the strength of his presence.

Chapter Seven

Judd glanced around the gathering crowd. He aimed to help the family cope, but most of all, he wanted to take the look of shock and sorrow from Madge's eyes.

He'd found Quint in the hayloft huddled to the wall, a cat nuzzled against him. The boy had understood his mother had died but didn't know how to react. He'd been grateful for something to do when Judd sent him to notify the neighbors.

Joanie seemed incapable of doing anything but clinging to Conrad, whose eyes were wide and unfocused.

Madge opened her arms and her heart to the younger girls and shepherded them through the day. She managed very well once she'd shaken her initial shock.

Watching her kindness convinced him his feelings

for her were growing ripe, ready to mature. Was it love? Whatever it was, he couldn't let it distract him from his reason for being here—George Gratton.

Madge crossed the yard and stood close to him. Sensing her need for reassurance and comfort, he squeezed her shoulders. She stiffened momentarily, then sighed and leaned closer. They broke apart in a heartbeat rather than cause gossip among the neighbors, but Judd hugged her shape and memory to him even though she now stood a circumspect twelve inches away. Seemed he needed her as much as he hoped she needed him.

More people arrived, and Madge moved off to welcome them. One of the neighbor men beckoned to Judd to ask him about the chores.

For the next two days their lives were like that— passing silently as they went from one task to another. Only the daily ride back to the Morgan place provided them with a chance to be alone, and then the conversation dealt with details of the Burns family.

As soon as they reached home, Madge hurriedly changed into her chore clothes—overalls and an old cotton shirt that must have been her father's. She rolled the sleeves up to her elbows and set to work. Despite her protests, he insisted on helping.

"I'll get the cow and calf."

She hesitated only a moment. "Thanks. I'll start

the washing." Several women held back on their regular orders, understanding Madge had her hands full helping the Burns family, but a couple insisted they must have clean laundry.

He brought home the cow and calf and did the milking. Not the sort of job a cowboy often did, but he discovered it surprisingly soothing to lean against the cow's flank as warm streams of milk filled the bucket. Sally took the pail when he carried it to the house.

Louisa sat at the table where they usually did their studies. "Justin, I wonder if you could help me with this lesson?"

He glanced over his shoulder. Madge had already put in a long day at the Burnses', serving neighbors, managing to do some laundry so the children would have clean clothes for the funeral tomorrow and helping Joanie and Mary keep the children occupied and the confusion organized. She must be worn out. He wanted to help her, but of course, Louisa was feeling neglected. So he buried his sigh. "Certainly. We can work until you're tired."

"I won't get tired very early. I napped all afternoon so I could do lessons this evening."

Yes, she napped while her sister slaved. Not that he had any right to resent the fact. Louisa wasn't strong like Madge. Strong and kind and helpful and independent—

He struggled to keep his thoughts on Louisa's lessons as Madge carted baskets of wet sheets upstairs to hang. If only he could stop pretending to be Justin, the schoolteacher, and be Judd, the rugged cowboy. Then he would have no qualms about refusing Louisa's request and helping Madge.

The funeral was the next day. Everyone hurried through morning work so they could be ready to go to the church right after lunch.

The building was crowded, the yard full of those who couldn't fit inside. Room had been reserved for the Morgans in the church but Judd remained outdoors.

The family followed the simple casket in, Joanie at Conrad's side, practically holding him up. Quint and Mary each held the hands of one of the younger girls.

Judd ducked his head at the sight of such grief and confusion.

Following the service and interment in the nearby graveyard, the ladies of the church set up a lunch. People filed by the family and offered condolences.

Quint slipped away, unnoticed by the others. Judd followed him to where the buggies were hitched. He dropped his arm across the boy's shoulders but said nothing. Simply was there for him.

Quint shuddered. "Why did God have to take my momma?"

"Son, I really don't know." Why did God allow such awful things to happen?

"She used to say plants need deep roots to survive. Said roots grew deep when the plants had to fight wind and drought and other bad stuff."

"Guess that's so." But plants didn't have hearts, feelings. They couldn't wonder why or resent the elements.

"Momma told me I'd be a better man for having to deal with hard things. Said God would help me through them."

"Your momma sounds like a wise woman."

"She was." He sucked in air. "But I don't like hard things."

Judd nodded. "Don't guess any of us do." He tried not to think of his own circumstances. Nor how God hadn't seemed concerned enough to help his mother.

"Momma would be disappointed in me if I didn't stand up like a man." The boy straightened and Judd's arm fell to his side.

"All of you have a heavy load to carry now."

Quint's shoulders sank. "I know." He pulled himself tall again. "But I aim to make Momma proud." He glanced toward the crowd around his older brother and sister. Saw the younger ones playing, unconcerned about the future. For a moment his gaze lingered on the little ones. Judd sensed he struggled with wanting to stay young and carefree like them, a child, then he looked back to Conrad and Mary. "I better go." His stride faltering only once, he returned to their side and faced the greetings of the neighbors.

Judd glanced about for Madge, found her surrounded by a knot of women. She seemed to be in a heated discussion. He slipped to her side.

She shot him a grateful glance as she continued to speak to one of the women. "I think it's up to Conrad and Mary to decide what happens to the younger girls."

Judd jerked his attention to the circle of ladies. "What's going on here?"

Only Madge seemed inclined to answer. "Some think Pearl and Rosie should be taken away."

"They need to be in a proper family," one of the women murmured. "Or the orphanage where they will be cared for."

Judd cleared his throat and gained their attention. "Aren't you forgetting they have a family? Would you deprive them of that after they've had the misfortune of losing their parents?"

Some women shuffled about, but the speaker wasn't convinced. "The older children are way too young to be parents."

"Conrad is eighteen. I venture to say many of you were married and had a baby by then."

"That's so," several acknowledged.

"But Mary is only fourteen."

Madge shook her head. "I can't believe we're having this conversation with the grave over there not even filled in."

Judd took her elbow, hoping to calm her. "My grandmother was but fourteen when she moved west as a newlywed. She didn't have a home to go to. She and her new husband had to build one with their own hands. They faced challenges most of us have forgotten about. Mary and Conrad, Quint and the little girls have each other. They have a warm home and a farm—"

"Farm is more of a burden than anything."

Judd went on as if he hadn't been interrupted. "They have a cow and chickens and a garden Mary has been responsible for for the past two years. They are family. They love Rosie and Pearl. They'd never consider them a burden or extra mouths to feed. I think if we are concerned about them we should do what we can to assist them."

One by one the women nodded agreement and moved off, except for the most vocal one who lingered a moment, then marched away.

"I hope she won't make trouble for them," Madge said, still clinging to his arm.

"I doubt she will if she doesn't have the support of anyone else."

She faced him. "You handled that very well. Thank you." Their gazes held and said so many things they had never confessed. Judd allowed himself to believe her lingering look echoed his own thoughts. Something special and real was developing between them.

"Madge." Mrs. Morgan quietly took her daughter's arm. "I need you."

Madge jerked her head to one side, avoiding Judd's eyes. "Of course, Mother."

As they edged away, Judd wondered what Mrs. Morgan said to cause Madge to nod and look regretful.

Over the next few days they all struggled to get back to their normal routines, but Judd found himself more and more restless—a feeling he could not explain. It was as if some inner, unidentified purpose drove him. He tried to force that nameless feeling into the shape of George Gratton but found it impossible. He scolded himself. He could not let sweet thoughts of Madge steal away his resolve to deal with the scoundrel. He'd bring Gratton to justice, then his heart and thoughts could seek after Madge.

Evenings he often accompanied her to town, but more and more, he waited and slipped away as Judd Kirk. George had moved in before Mrs. Burns's funeral. Judd watched the house, seeing the man cooking his own meal, sitting at the chair reading or sometimes standing on the porch enjoying the air.

Judd wondered whom he intended to take advantage of in this town. Whomever and whatever Gratton had in mind, Judd planned to find out and reveal it before anyone was duped. It would require patient observation for the right timing. Judd would have to wait for the man to reveal his hand enough that he could be proven the shyster he was.

Over supper that night, Madge barely waited for them to all be served before she spilled her news. "I met Mr. Gratton today. You know, the man I cleaned the Sterling house for. He asked if I would be willing to work two afternoons a week for him."

"Of course, you agreed to," Louisa said. "Seems you are always looking for more work."

Louisa's voice was gentle, but Judd sensed an unkind dig. From the hurt flitting across Madge's eyes, he knew she felt it, too.

"I'm only trying to earn enough to pay some bills."

He wondered why she didn't lay the truth before them—if not for her hard work, they might lose their home. He supposed she wanted to protect them from worry.

"Anyway, what I really wanted to tell you was what a nice man he is."

Judd's heart twisted so hard he clenched his fists to keep from protesting.

"He thanked me for doing such a good job of cleaning the house, then asked me if I could make a meal or two a week for him. I told him I wasn't as good a cook as my sister, Sally, but he said he was willing to give it a try. Then he asked if I thought the small parlor could be made into a bedroom. He's planning to move his mother in with him, and she's apparently not well enough to be going up and down stairs. I said I thought it would suit very well, so he wants me to prepare it for her."

"How good God is to provide you with another job," Mrs. Morgan said. "Perhaps you can give up some of your laundry customers now."

"I don't think so, Mother."

"I can help with the laundry," Sally offered.

The sisters studied each other for several seconds. Judd guessed Madge had grown used to seeing her sisters as frail and unsuitable for heavy work. Madge needed to see Sally was no longer a little sister needing protection. He sensed Louisa was also far stronger than any of them were willing to believe.

Finally Madge nodded. "I'd appreciate your help."

Judd was pleased for Madge's sake. At the same time, he wanted to grab her and warn her not to take George Gratton at face value. Was the man figuring to gain something from his contact with

Madge? Perhaps to be introduced to Mrs. Morgan? But the woman had nothing to steal. Of course, Mr. Gratton didn't know that. Or perhaps this woman he planned to bring to the house was not truly his mother. Maybe she was part of some scheme he had cooked up.

Judd simply couldn't believe the man wasn't working some angle.

Having Madge at the Sterling house two afternoons a week forced Judd to be a lot more careful about watching the place. She often stayed to clean up the evening meal, forcing Judd to stay out of sight until she left for home.

He was caught between avoiding her and wanting to spend every moment with her.

The next day, Sally handed Madge a covered dish hot from the oven. "Would you take this to the Burns family? And see if they need anything."

Madge hesitated. "The laundry."

"There's only some sheets to iron. I'll look after that. They know you better than me. They'd rather see you."

Madge nodded. "I'll go. I've been wondering about them." She headed out to the car.

Judd rose. "I'll come along, if you don't mind."

Madge stopped midstride. She turned slowly. He followed her glance around the room. Why did

Louisa purse her lips and Mrs. Morgan send some kind of silent warning to Madge? Had they taken note of his evening absences and wondered if he conducted some shameful business? He wished he could assure them such was not the case, but he couldn't. Not without revealing far too much of his true identity. "I'd like to see how Quint is doing and the rest of the family, too, of course."

Another silent message passed between Madge and her mother, then Madge nodded. "Of course you must reassure yourself as to how they're doing."

So a few minutes later he sat beside her in the car, the succulent aroma of the hot dish filling the interior. Even though he'd already eaten, his taste buds were tempted.

He wanted to say things from his heart, but Madge quickly began to fill in the silence. After a few minutes of listening to her chatter, he decided she was purposely making it impossible for him to speak of anything important, and he settled back to listen. He would get a chance. He'd see to it. He had it on his mind to tell her how his affection for her was developing. Hopefully she would admit similar feelings.

His teeth stung as she talked of her growing regard for Mr. Gratton. She'd be shocked and dismayed to learn he was the man Judd wanted to bring to justice, but she'd understand when Gratton revealed his true colors. Meanwhile, he needed to concentrate on what she said.

"Joanie hoped Conrad would see this was a good time to ask her to marry him. They've been together since they were fourteen. But no, he says it wouldn't be honoring his mother's memory if he tried to replace her so soon. Pshaw. Mrs. Burns would be the first to agree Connie has waited long enough. The whole family would benefit from having Connie married. 'Twould stop the old ladies in town from grumbling about the two little girls needing a proper home."

"They're still at that? I thought they'd have let it drop by now."

She laughed. "You mean after you set them straight at the funeral?"

"I figured I made my point very clear."

"Oh, you did, indeed." She sobered much too quickly. "Some people aren't happy unless they are stirring up trouble."

"Does Conrad know about this?"

"Joanie told him. Thought it would persuade him to reconsider, but he said it wouldn't be fair to expect her to take over so much responsibility. Said they would manage as they were and no one would be taking his little sisters."

"No reason they should." The idea of someone trying made him as angry as hearing Gratton had stolen his mother's savings. "Where is the justice in this world?"

She slowed the car to look at him. "Judd, you showed justice when you defended the family and when you stood by them after their mother's death. We see glimpses of justice every day. Or maybe, more importantly, we see evidence of mercy. God's mercy."

"How is that evident in the drought?"

"Even in the drought He has not forsaken us. I believe the fact I am able to find feed for the cow and her calf, or earn enough money to pay the mortgage, is surely evidence of God's continuing care."

"I suppose I don't have your kind of faith."

"What kind do you have?" She held his gaze, demanding, searching.

He wanted to look away but found he couldn't. He wanted to throw all his doubts out the window and believe as he once had—before he'd drifted so far away, before he'd decided he would see Gratton pay for his deeds.

For a moment he wrestled with the promise of peace in trusting everything to God versus the need to exact his own form of justice. But he could not let the man get away with what he'd done. Somehow Gratton must pay and, above all, be prevented from repeating his sly tricks.

They approached the Burnses' farm, providing him an excuse to deflect her question. "We're here."

She flicked him a disappointed look but let the subject go as she drove up the lane to the house. Two little girls burst from the door and rushed to the car to hug Madge and give Judd shy smiles. Mary came to the doorway. "Welcome. Come in." She looked much better than when he'd seen her at the funeral. In fact, she was a pretty little thing. He suspected Conrad would not have her as surrogate mother for many years. Long enough perhaps to see the little ones able to cope on their own—or perhaps Conrad would come to his senses and marry Joanie.

"Is Quint about?"

"He's out with Connie trying to put up some hay."

"Thanks." He wondered where they would find enough grass to provide hay for the winter. He found them in a low spot behind the barn, cutting Russian thistle and packing it into a stack. The thistle was thorny and difficult to work with. Even though they wore leather guards on their legs and arms, both were scratched and bleeding.

If Madge saw this, she would surely change her mind about justice and mercy.

Seeing him, they eagerly abandoned the job. "We'll finish later," Conrad said to Quint. "It's a wonder we found this patch before it dried up and blew away. It will go a long ways toward feeding the milk cow over the winter."

Thorny thistles hardly qualified as a blessing in Judd's opinion, which he decided he'd keep to himself.

Quint seemed to have grown several inches. Judd realized it was because the boy stood straight and tall.

"You're looking better, apart from all the scratches," Judd said.

"Feeling better, thanks. I forgot for a little while that God will not abandon us. Connie told me the last thing Momma asked him to do was read a Bible verse. We're all going to memorize it and remember it when we get discouraged."

"That's great." Madge would be so glad to hear it. He wished again his faith were so clear and strong.

"I don't know if I've got it a hundred percent right, but this is it, Psalm sixty-eight, verse five, 'A father of the fatherless, and a judge of the widows, is God in His holy habitation.'"

Conrad squeezed Quint's shoulder. "God will take care of our every need. Isn't that what Momma always taught us?"

Quint nodded, his eyes filled with trust. "Yes, she did. And I don't aim to forget."

Both of them shed their leather guards and torn

shirts. Conrad noticed Judd's curiosity. "We don't want to upset the girls." They put on fresh shirts.

They trooped to the house for tea and cookies. Madge and Mary laughed at something as Judd and the boys stepped into the kitchen. Then Madge gave the girl a quick hug. She glanced over Mary's shoulder, saw Judd, and her eyes seemed to smile deeper, happier, as if she were glad to see him.

His steps faltered. He saw her more clearly than ever before. She had an incredible capacity to love, to believe the best in people, to encourage others and to fight for what was right.

It made her see George Gratton as the man wanted to be seen—a good man with noble purposes.

Judd counted on her sense of justice to make her see the man for what he truly was when Judd revealed the truth.

Madge broke away from the intensity of their locked gaze and waved toward the table.

As soon as everyone was seated, Conrad cleared his throat. "Let's say grace over our blessings." He reached his hand toward Mary on one side and Quint on the other. Quint reached for Judd's hand. Judd had no choice but to reach for Madge's.

Their gazes met and held in an electric burst that consumed the distance separating them and erased awareness of the others. For an eternal moment all that existed was each other and raw honest feelings between them, then she bowed her head.

His head bowed, he struggled to find solid ground for his thoughts and feelings.

Conrad prayed a simple prayer. Judd opened his eyes, uncertain where to look. His feelings were too strong to let the others guess at them. Looking at Madge would certainly make them more difficult to control. But he couldn't stop himself from a quick peek in her direction. Had she felt the same shuddering, overwhelming sensation?

But as her glance touched him, then went on to Mary without a spark of anything out of the ordinary, he sucked back disappointment. Seemed he was the only one who had felt the zing between them.

She turned her attention to the tea and cookies, and a short time later, Madge and Judd left, promising to visit again soon.

"They're doing okay, I think," Madge said. "Better than I thought they would." Such ordinary words. Had she really been unaware of the sparks between them that almost seared his skin?

"They'll do just fine if it depends on them. However, so much depends on crops, rain, prices and a thousand things they have no control over."

"But God is in control. I asked you earlier what kind of faith you have. You didn't answer."

He should have known she wouldn't forget. He

considered his words carefully. "Madge, I once had a simple faith. Childlike. Then life got complicated."

"In what way?"

"I'm not sure I can explain."

"Try. I truly want to understand."

Because she cared and because he wanted her acceptance, he tried to shape his vague thoughts into some sort of sense. "I left teaching because I found it boring and headed west to ranching country. Out there a man lives or dies, fails or succeeds, by his own strength. He counts on only his own wits. I never saw any need of God's help. Then my mother lost everything, despite her unfaltering faith. All I could think to do was what I'd learned in the west country—take care of the business myself."

"But where did faith enter the picture?"

"You mean did I consult God? I didn't. Seems His hands are more than full with trying to fix the problems of the world."

"You're suggesting He's falling down on the job?"

He hadn't meant for his tone to reveal his doubts, but her words pretty much explained how he felt. "When I see how the Burns family is coping, I am amazed. It almost makes me wish I had their simple faith."

"Their 'simple faith,' as you call it, has been birthed through loss and disappointment, and thrived and strengthened through more adversity."

"Quint told me about trees…plants…needing wind and storms to grow deep roots."

"That sounds like something Mrs. Burns would say."

Judd stared out the window. His self-sufficiency sounded rootless and weak when compared to the Burnses'. But he didn't know how to change. He'd lived life on his own terms too long. Perhaps Madge realized that and despised it. But he couldn't change who he was. Wouldn't even consider it until George Gratton received proper justice.

A sign, weather-beaten and almost buried in drifted soil, caught his attention. "Does that say For Sale?"

"Yes. The old Cotton place."

"What's it like?"

"Nice enough, though it's been empty almost two years. Do you want to see it?"

"I'd like to."

She jerked to a halt and reversed to the turnoff. "I hope we can get through." Soil had blown over the trail in many places, but she managed to plow through it until they reached the farmyard.

"Let's look around." Something inside him quickened at the stately two-story house, the hip-roofed barn, the row of smaller outbuildings. "Buildings appear solid."

"Mr. Cotton spared no expense. Borrowed heavily. Now he's gone."

They stepped around dirt drifts to the house. He tried the door. It opened with a grating squeal. "They even left some furniture."

"They took only what they could carry with them. The bank claimed the rest."

He stepped into the room that had served as kitchen. "A good size." One door led to a pantry, another to a generous-size room complete with table, chairs and sideboard. The third door—with double-wide sliding panels—led to the front room and off that was a bedroom or parlor or whatever need it suited. "This is fantastic. Why isn't someone living here?"

"Who can afford to buy it?"

"Let's go upstairs." Four bedrooms and a roomy closet opened off the hallway. He couldn't get over the beautiful house standing vacant.

They returned outside and explored the rest of the buildings. Struggling trees stood behind the house.

A restless yearning grew in Judd's heart. "I could see myself living here."

She watched him. "No money in farming."

He caught her chin and gazed deep into her eyes, seeing the willingness and promises he ached for and feared he would not see. "I could do something else until the economy turned around."

A flare of interest crossed her face. "I thought you wanted to go back to ranching."

"I've never had a reason to consider anything else." His fingers rested on her chin. She made no move to put distance between them. For days he'd ached for a chance to be alone with her, share the truth of his growing fondness for her. "Now staying here seems pretty alluring."

Tiny smile lines creased the edges of her eyes as she correctly interpreted his words to mean the allure was to more than an empty farm.

"I could see myself putting down roots in this place, especially with someone special to share it with."

She swallowed hard. Her eyelids flickered downward, then jerked up to reveal deep longings.

He caught his breath. "Madge." Slowly, anticipating each second of preparation, he lowered his head, tipping her chin a little so their lips touched gently, clung briefly. He wanted more. Everything. All of her forever. He wanted to share his life, his heart, his dreams, his all. Longing made his kiss grow more urgent.

"No." She pushed back, shoulders heaving in frantic gasps. "No. I can't do this." She spun around and raced away.

"Madge. What on earth?" He caught her in three strides and pulled her to a halt. She fought him, batting at his hands, rolling her head back and forth. He would not release her. Not without an explanation.

"What's wrong? It was just a little kiss."

She broke free again and backed away, her eyes wide, her lips pressed tight. She looked ready to cry.

His heart cracked with concern, and he reached for her. "Madge, whatever it is, I'm sure we can fix it."

She kept a safe distance between them. "No, we can't. You. Me." She shook her head. "No. Louisa—" She broke off and clamped her lips tight. Stubbornness hardened her eyes.

"What about Louisa?"

"Nothing. Only that you are supposed to be her tutor."

"I am her tutor. What does that have to do with you and me? You aren't making sense."

She headed for the car. "Doesn't matter. You and I just can't be."

He grabbed her arm again. "I deserve more than that." At least he liked to think he did.

Her eyes suggested she wanted to explain. But she said, "I simply can't tell you more." She left him standing ankle-deep in a brown drift.

What secret could she be hiding to make love between them impossible?

A niggling doubt made its way to the surface of his thoughts. Was her rejection because of his duplicity in continuing to pose as Justin Bellamy? Did her strong morals make him an undeserving suitor because of his continued quest for justice?

If so, he must somehow convince her he was correct in his stand. The best way would be to prove Gratton's evilness as soon as possible.

Madge waited for him at the car.

"Go ahead. I'll walk the rest of the way. I need time to think."

She closed her eyes and sucked in air.

His heart seemed to beat thick syrup. Whatever her reasons, he was not mistaken in thinking her decision hurt her as much as it did him.

He would find an answer to this unnamed problem before it tore them both apart.

Chapter Eight

Madge forced her heavy limbs into the car and grabbed the steering wheel. She sat for a moment, unable to think what she meant to do. *Start the car.* She did. *Head for home.* She aimed the car down the trail.

By the time she reached the main road, her shock gave way to weeping, and she pulled to the side and pressed her face to the back of her hands, letting tears drip over the spokes of the steering wheel.

His kiss had been the sweetest thing in the world, making her forget everything but his arms about her, his presence in her heart and the way her whole being wanted to belong to him.

What was she going to do? She pulled her head up. Perhaps if she spoke to Mother, explained how she felt…

She must try. She couldn't live with this war of

longing and guilt inside. Nor could she let herself care for Judd without Mother's approval.

She lifted her head and snorted. As if she could hope to keep herself from caring. She thought of him with every breath, dreamed of him in every dream. Touring the old Cotton place, she'd thought of sharing each room with him, filling it with their love and hard work.

She'd speak to Mother as soon as she got back home, and if she gave the answer Madge hoped for, she would explain everything to Judd when he returned.

Louisa watched at the window as Madge slid from the car. She could tell Louisa wasn't pleased. The tight set of her lips made Madge's blood scrape through her veins.

Perhaps, before the next hour was out, Louisa would be reconciled to Judd caring for Madge.

Wasn't she always telling Judd to trust God to do what was right? Now was the time to practice what she preached. *Lord God, please make things work out.* She relaxed marginally.

"Hello, Louisa," she said cheerfully as she stepped into the room.

"What have you done with Justin?"

Madge pressed her lips together. Was it so obvious they had kissed?

"Why didn't he come back with you?"

Oh. Only that. "I left him a mile or two down the road. He decided he wanted to walk."

Louisa perked up. "Have you two had a spat?"

"No. Where's Mother?"

"In the other room. Why?" Louisa's voice demanded answers.

"I just want to speak to her." She headed for the front room. When Louisa started to follow, Madge said, "It's private."

Pretty Louisa marred her looks with a scowl fit for a banker about to lose his last penny. "You're up to something. And I think it involves Justin. Which means it involves me."

"If it does I'll be sure to notify you." She crossed the threshold and pulled the door closed after her.

Mother sat before the radio listening to a program. She glanced at Madge, then reached over to turn the knob off. "What is it?"

She sat by her mother and sought for the words to explain. "Mother, what do you think about Justin?"

"He seems a fine young man. He and Louisa have a lot in common. And hasn't Louisa's health improved with his attention?"

"Louisa appears fond of him, doesn't she?" She knew the answer but hoped—prayed—mother would have seen it differently.

"I'm happy with how their relationship is progressing. Why do you ask?"

"I just wonder—" Wanting the man chosen for her sister was downright selfish. "Does Justin know your ultimate goal concerning him?"

"I haven't said anything yet. It seemed premature."

"Don't you think he should? Besides, what do you really know about him?"

"Having him here every day gives us a good chance to assess his character."

Madge didn't respond. Justin wasn't even real, yet Mother and Louisa thought he was the right man for the eldest sister. "I think you should ask him about his past, his plans for the future. Maybe it's time to see what his interest in Louisa is."

Louisa burst through the door. "You're trying to steal him from me. Isn't it enough that you have good health while mine is poor? Or that you get to do the things you want? Seems you just can't stand to see me get anything before you do, even though I'm older."

Madge stared at her. Sweet Louisa revealing such venom? Hardly seemed possible. "I'm not trying to steal anything from you." She hoped her guilty secret of a stolen kiss didn't send telltale pink to her cheeks.

"Then where is he? Why do you take him with you, then leave him to find his own way home?" She turned to Mother. "She left him to walk. Poor

Justin with his bad leg. He'll be coughing all night after this."

It was all Madge could do not to snort in disbelief. "He'll be fine."

"Well, I'm concerned." The look she gave Madge told of a care beyond thinking of him walking a mile or two.

Madge smiled gently. "You have no reason to worry." She would not be guilty of taking what her sister wanted and deserved. She glanced at Mother, wanting to say more, wanting to urge her to question Justin more closely, assess his interest.

Mother watched Madge and Louisa with wise knowing.

Madge shifted her attention to the far corner of the room. She did not want Mother to guess at her heart's yearning. If only Mother would question Judd, ascertain the truth, then perhaps both she and Louisa would change their minds about the man.

But until that happened, Madge would avoid him.

She bid them good-night and hurried up the stairs to crumple on her bed. Somehow she'd expected this to turn out differently. Didn't God see her heart? Know her affection for Judd? But Louisa cared about him, too. No, she cared about Justin. If this deception continued, Louisa was going to be hurt badly when she discovered Justin wasn't real. Or maybe Judd wasn't real.

She touched her lips, remembering their recent kiss, and smiled. Oh, Judd was real enough. And the way she'd felt holding his hand at the Burnses' place was further proof.

What was she to do? Could she persuade Judd to tell the truth? Or encourage Mother to probe and discover it herself?

She flipped to her back and stared at the ceiling. Shouldn't she trust God to order things rightly? But what if she left the situation in God's hands and Louisa and Justin—or would he be Judd?—married? Could she still trust God?

Sometimes it was so very difficult not to take things into her own hands.

Madge was beginning to really welcome the afternoons spent at the Gratton house. Mr. Gratton usually came home before she left. They often worked together before she served his supper and headed home.

He had a narrow bed moved into the room they were converting for his mother. At her suggestion, he put in a chiffonier and a wardrobe. Madge hung pictures, made up the bed and draped a colorful quilt over the foot.

"It looks welcoming," George—as he'd instructed Madge to call him—said. "Thank you for making it so."

"It was fun." Even more importantly, working here got her away from home and provided an escape from Judd. When she left each afternoon, he still sat with Louisa. She hoped his instruction was confined to Greek and art and didn't include lessons on romance.

He'd glanced up more than once as she crossed the yard carrying a basket of clean articles but couldn't offer to help her with the laundry deliveries, as he'd still been with Louisa. That had been her intention.

She shifted her attention back to George. "What's your mother like?"

"She's not as strong as she used to be, though she'd never admit it. Wait, I'll get a picture." He thumped up the stairs and returned with a small likeness of a lady with silver hair and a direct look. There was a strong family resemblance.

"She looks sweet," Madge commented.

He chuckled. "Sweet and determined. Tell me about your family."

She told of her sisters and described their life in quick detail.

"No beau?"

She hesitated. Wished she could deny it. But she couldn't admit it, either. "No," she said.

"I sense there's more to it."

"I care about a man, but he's not for me."

"Who is he for, then?"

"For another. One more worthy and deserving." She tried to believe it, but a stubborn bit of defensiveness argued Judd would find Louisa far too soft and needy.

"My dear, any man who would think that isn't worthy of you."

His kind words brought a sting to her eyes. She wished she could explain Judd hadn't suggested such a thing.

George wisely dropped the subject. "I have a few family mementos to put out. Would you help me?" He brought in a box. They set out family pictures and hung some paintings—only copies but still lovely. Then he pulled out a crystal bowl. The light struck it, sending flickers of color across the room.

Madge caught her breath. "It's beautiful." She could picture it full of truffles or Christmas oranges. Or sitting on a crocheted doily. She put it in the center of the table—she'd find a doily later. Would the table abandoned at the Cotton farm clean up as nicely as this one had? She rubbed the polished surface. Not that she had anything like this crystal bowl to put on it. The floors at the farm looked as if a good cleaning would fix them, but the old wallpaper would have to come down.

She closed her eyes, pushing away such useless dreams. George moved to her side, staring at the bowl.

"It's all I have left of my former life. Alas, like

many, I over invested in the market. Got too bold and, I suppose, too greedy. Lost everything. To my sorrow, I lost more than my own."

"I'm sorry."

"It taught me a lesson…don't trust in things that can be so easily lost."

Trust. She'd never found it as difficult to trust God as she did now. Would He make it possible for her to love Judd, or…she could barely breathe…would He provide the strength for her to watch Louisa marry him?

"Sometimes—" her voice was a mere whisper "—it's hard to rest in God."

"True, my dear. But easier than taking matters into our own hands and having to deal with watching things crumble before our eyes."

She sensed personal, raw experience behind his words, but they were wise comfort. She'd trust God to work things out.

It was late when she finally headed home. Truth was, home no longer felt like a place of safety and shelter. She feared she would encounter Judd at every turn and had come to dread Louisa's dark glances. If George had invited her to stay and share his meal she would have done so gladly, but he seemed to expect she'd want to hurry back to her family.

She'd purposely delayed her return until she was certain supper would be over when she arrived. Sally had left food in the oven for her. Although she wasn't hungry, she pulled the plate out and sat down to eat. Mother came from the front room to join her.

"Where's Louisa and Sally?" Madge asked.

"Sally has gone to visit friends. Louisa is in bed."

"In bed?" That was three days in a row she'd retired early. "Is she sick?" Or pointedly avoiding Madge?

Mother's hands moved restlessly across the table. "She's begged for an afternoon nap the last two days."

That wasn't a good sign. "I thought—" She assumed once Madge backed off, Louisa would grow closer to Justin. Actually, she'd hoped Justin would tell her the truth about who he was, and Louisa would—what? Did Madge really think Louisa would see Judd as less attractive than Justin? "Has she argued with Justin?"

"Not to my knowledge."

"Do you think we should ask the doctor to call?" To her shame, she mentally counted the pennies the visit would cost.

"I don't know. It isn't like she has a fever or complains of any pain. Let's wait a few more days."

The next day Madge pushed aside her desire to avoid Judd in order to observe Louisa. She paused going up the stairs with laundry to watch the pair.

Judd read from a textbook. Louisa stared out the window, her mind certainly not on the studies. That alone was more than enough evidence Louisa was sick.

A few minutes later Madge returned, and when she glanced in the room, she saw Louisa with her head back and her eyes closed. Either she was ill or had overtaxed herself with too much studying.

Madge made sure she was at the table for supper, even though it took every scrap of self-control to keep her gaze away from Judd. Not that she needed to look his way to note his ink-stained hands reach for a bowl of potatoes. Hadn't he said he hated teaching? Her nerves crackled in response to the tension emanating from him. Was he resenting the time he spent tutoring Louisa? Had Louisa guessed? Perhaps that explained the way she picked at her food.

Whatever the cause, Madge determined to get to the bottom of it. As soon as Judd left for the evening, she would speak to Louisa.

Judd didn't linger. Madge tried to convince herself she didn't regret the fact, but part of her followed him across the yard. Would he change into Judd clothes and go to town? Would she see him there?

She curtly cut off such thoughts and headed to the front room where Louisa lay on the sofa, her head on a pillow, a blanket wrapped around her. Madge edged a chair close and sat down. "Louisa, what's wrong with you?"

Louisa's eyes flew open, and Madge blinked before the anger she saw. "Besides never having any energy and always having to take whatever scraps people toss my way? Why, nothing, dear sister. Nothing."

The accusations burned a hole in Madge's heart. "Louisa, that's not fair. I don't do that. I've always helped you as best I could."

Louisa looked ready to cry. "I know you do. I'm sorry. I'm just feeling such a burden to everyone."

Madge knelt beside the couch and pulled Louisa into her arms. "You're my sister. You could never be a burden."

Louisa shivered. "Even if I took the man you love?"

Madge stiffened. Were her feelings so obvious? She'd tried her best to hide them. She forced a little laugh. "Can you see us falling in love with the same man? I can't. You'd want someone kind and gentle and interested in studies." Like Justin. "I'd want someone bold, adventuresome, hardworking." Like Judd. Oh, what a muddle.

"No one will ever love me. I'm too much bother."

That brought a genuine laugh from Madge. "You need to clean your mirror so you see the beautiful girl there next time you look in it."

"You think I am?"

Madge pushed away to grin at her sister. "Louisa, I'm the workhorse and you're the beauty. If you weren't my beloved sister, I'd be jealous."

Louisa laughed. "And if you weren't my sister, I'd be jealous of how hard you work."

"Don't ever wish to trade places with me."

"Sometimes I do."

"Oh, no, dear sister, never." How could she harbor selfish thoughts when Louisa was so generous?

Louisa sat up and faced Madge. "I could not bear if something came between us. Especially if it was my fault."

"That will never happen." Madge vowed not to be guilty of creating a rift between them. If Louisa loved Judd and he learned to love her...and why wouldn't he? As she said, Louisa was the beautiful one.

They talked sister stuff for a few minutes, then Madge left to make her deliveries, more convinced than ever not to interfere with Mother's plans for Louisa and Justin.

She dropped off laundry at two places, picked up more to wash at two other places and decided to drive past the Gratton house before she headed home. Maybe George would be on the porch and she could stop for a visit. She found a great deal of comfort from his wise words.

But he wasn't outside. The only light was in the front room. She glimpsed him sitting in an armchair reading. She had no right to disturb him.

A shadow separated from the fence, and she stared as it turned into Judd. Was he waiting for her? Hoping to catch a ride home?

She could not bear the thought of being sequestered with him in the tiny space of the car, filled as it was with so many memories, so she pretended not to notice him and sped on by.

Madge hoped her little talk with Louisa would make her feel better. She purposely avoided Judd as much as possible, thinking Louisa would take heart. It stung more than Madge cared to admit to snub him, especially when she caught a flash of confusion on his face. She didn't know what else to do. Seemed every choice she made hurt someone. She prayed long and hard, but her prayers yielded no change— not in her heart nor in the situation between Louisa and Justin.

Despite all she did to help her sister, Louisa grew more and more morose. Finally, Mother called a family meeting. "Louisa, I've consulted both Sally and Madge and have their full agreement. We don't like to see you going downhill this way. I've decided to ask the doctor to visit. Perhaps he can suggest a tonic or something." The worry in Mother's voice spoke for all of them.

Louisa bolted upright in her chair. "No, Mother. It's not necessary. My ailment isn't something the doctor can give me a prescription for."

"You can't go on this way."

Louisa seemed to fight an internal battle, then she nodded. "You are quite right. It's time I fixed things." She pushed from the table. "I need to be alone to work things out and then I'll take the action I need." As regal as a queen, she left the room.

Mother, Sally and Madge stared after her.

"What on earth?" Mother asked. "What is she talking about?"

"I don't know," Madge said. Sally echoed her words.

But they didn't have to wait long to find out. Louisa returned an hour later with a quiet determination in her expression.

"Are you okay, dear?" Mother asked.

"I'm fine." Louisa's voice was firm, and she sat down and opened a book.

Madge waited until Mother went outside to help Sally in the garden to approach her sister. "Louisa, what's going on?"

Louisa smiled. "I've been guilty of feeling sorry for myself and worse, but I've repented and I intend to correct my behavior."

Madge opened her mouth twice—once to protest, but no words would form, and a second time to demand specifics.

"That's between myself and God," Louisa said—and she would say nothing more.

Finally, in frustration, Madge gave up prodding her sister. "I have no idea what you think you've done, but so long as you've dealt with it and can stop moping about...all I want is for you to be happy."

Louisa nodded, her expression serious. "I want the same for you."

Madge nodded. She'd never questioned Louisa's love, just as she hoped Louisa would never have cause to question hers.

Chapter Nine

Judd sat beside Louisa in their customary place. He struggled to keep his thoughts on the lesson he'd prepared, but it proved a challenge, especially when Louisa looked for her usual keen attention. "I've heard good things about the play, *Deacon Dubbs,* that the community of Bowwell is putting on." Louisa mentioned a town almost an hour's drive away.

Judd murmured a noncommittal sound. Louisa had made her interest in him quite plain. He'd done his best to make it equally as clear that his interest lay elsewhere—on her sister.

"Madge has mentioned she'd like to see it."

Judd grunted. He had no idea what Louisa meant.

"She might go if you invited her."

"What?" He stared at innocent-looking eyes. "I hardly think so. She finds it impossible to even be in the same room as me." The way she jumped up and escaped if he entered the kitchen hurt like pouring kerosene on an open wound—one of his grandfather's favorite medical treatments. Once he'd thought she seemed as eager to spend time together as he was.

Until he'd kissed her.

"I can't see how it would hurt to ask her." Louisa studied him with demanding eyes. "Unless you object to a little outing with her."

Object? Not in this lifetime. Did Louisa mean to encourage him in Madge's direction after the way she had hinted at her own interest? "Let me see if I understand you correctly. You're suggesting I ask Madge to accompany me to this play?"

"Just a thought," Louisa murmured.

Louisa's encouragement convinced him he should try again with Madge.

But finding a chance and constructing the right words proved a challenge as she continued to avoid him.

Finally, he decided to combine two things. He would study the Gratton house as he did most evenings, only this time he planned to show up when Madge prepared to leave, providing him a chance to talk to her.

That evening he waited, leaning against the car door, and watched her approach as she left the house.

She didn't see him at first. When she did, she faltered and glanced over her shoulder as if planning to seek refuge inside the Gratton house.

"You've been avoiding me. Why?"

She shook her head. "I'm not." As if to prove him wrong, she took two steps closer.

"You're sure of that?" He kept his arms crossed and continued to lounge against the car, although every nerve in his body ached to reach for her, pull her against his chest and breathe in her sweetness.

"Sure, I'm sure."

"Care to prove it?"

She backed up so fast he feared she'd fall.

He realized she'd interpreted his words as a challenge to a kiss. He hadn't meant them that way, though he had no objection to it. He quickly pulled his thoughts back to reality. "If you don't object to my company, then come with me to the play in Bowwell."

"A play?"

Did she sound disappointed? "I heard *Deacon Duff* is playing. Supposed to be a good play."

"Deacon Duff?"

Why did she seem so confused? He'd wanted to allow her a chance to say no, but now he couldn't bear the thought. "Let's make a day of it. We'll go in time to have supper. I think you'd enjoy the play. What do you think?" *Say yes.*

"I really can't."

"Why? Are you afraid to take time away from work?" At the stubborn denial on her face, he pressed his point. "Shouldn't trusting God mean a person can relax once in a while?"

"Of course I can relax."

"Then you'll come with me?"

"Fine. I'll go." She sounded as if he'd forced her into a corner and her agreement was out of necessity.

He wished he could see her better, but dusk had fallen and her face was shadowed. He moved closer, searching her expression. When he saw her tiny smile, he relaxed. She didn't seem to mind the idea at all.

They picked Friday as the night they would go.

He held the car door for Madge and bent over to the open window as he closed it. "I'll see you later."

"You could ride home with me." She smiled, then ducked her head, as if she didn't want him to see her expression.

He fought the urge to catch her chin, tip her face and assure himself he'd seen a flash of eager welcome. Judd considered accepting a ride with her, but he still hoped Gratton would reveal his hand. Perhaps tonight someone would come calling under cover of darkness, or Gratton might now set out to meet someone—most likely a lonesome widow woman with a secret stash of cash. "I'll be along later."

He stepped back so she could drive away. And he started counting the hours until they headed to Bowwell.

Friday finally arrived. He wished he'd asked her to leave right after lunch, but she would likely have demurred, claiming she had work to do. He watched her scurry around in order to do the laundry before it was time to go.

Louisa noticed his distraction. "Seems she could use some help if she's to take most of the afternoon away from her work. Which is a great idea, as far as I'm concerned. She works far too hard."

"Yes, she does." He tried to force his attention back to Greek conjugations. Somehow the whole language was clear as mud.

"Someone should help her," Louisa said.

"Uh-huh."

Louisa stared hard at him.

"Me?"

"I doubt I'd be of much use."

He tried to guess if Louisa had some ulterior motive, for her suggestion but her eyes were guileless. A small smile tugged at the corners of her mouth. He stared at her. She met his study without blinking. But her suggestion confused him. A few days ago she would have clung to him, fretting she'd never learn all she wanted without his help. She seemed to resent any time he spent pursuing other activities, especially if they involved Madge. Now if he didn't know better, he would suspect her of playing matchmaker.

Not that he was about to object.

"You're sure you don't mind?"

"I wouldn't suggest it if I did."

He slammed the book shut, apologized for the sharp noise and then hurried away without giving her a chance to say anything. Her laughter followed him out the door.

Madge had finished rinsing the sheets. He grabbed the basket.

"What are you doing?"

"I'll carry this up the stairs for you." Before she could open her mouth or dream up a protest, he clattered up the steps.

At first Madge didn't move, then she raced up after him. "Aren't you supposed to be teaching Louisa?"

"She kindly gave me the rest of the afternoon off."

Madge squinted at him. "She did, did she? Now, why would she do that?"

"'Cause she's afraid you won't get your work done in time to get ready, maybe?"

"She is?" She turned and grabbed a wet sheet and pegged it in place.

He ducked under the line so he could face her. "You seem surprised." No more than he had been.

"It seems odd to think of Louisa passing up a moment of lesson time."

"Do you question every kindness?"

She wrinkled her nose, but before she could voice an argument he let the sheet fall between them. He didn't intend to analyze Louisa's generous offer. The afternoon ahead promised all sorts of fun and delights that had nothing to do with the play they planned to see.

He returned outside to empty the wash water, carefully applying it to the growing plants. Despite the damage inflicted by the grasshoppers, there would be potatoes and carrots, beets, onions and even some chard, which he had developed a fondness for since coming to the Morgan household. As he headed back for the rest of the water, he glanced up and caught Madge watching him. He grinned and nodded. She blushed as bright as the combs on the chickens pecking in the yard and ducked out of sight.

Yes, it promised to be a fine day.

He hung the tubs to dry, then hurried to get ready. He wanted to go as Judd but wasn't sure how he could accomplish it without giving away his disguise. Only one way to do it. He waited for Madge to come down with the baskets ready to deliver. "Put them in my automobile. We'll take it."

Her eyes widened in surprise and—dare he think—delight.

"I'll drive up to the door of my shack and wait for you in the car."

As she realized what he intended, a becoming pink filled her cheeks. Just like a summer rose. "You're going as Judd," she murmured.

"Can't imagine enjoying the day any other way." He could never think of himself as Justin when he was with her.

He drove his car close to the soddie, then hurried into clothes that fit and boots that made him feel real. He only wished he could shave off the beard, but not yet. Instead, he trimmed it well, then, carrying his hat under his arm, he slipped into the car, hoping no one would take note of the difference in his appearance. He had only a moment to wait before Madge rushed across the yard wearing a dark blue dress with a white collar that made her eyes look as brown as pure chocolate. She'd brushed her hair back and held it in place with shiny combs.

His tongue grew thick at her beauty. Keeping his thoughts and emotions under control might well turn the afternoon into delightful torture.

He wanted to spring out and open the door for her, but, afraid her sisters and mother would be watching from the house, he sat as she climbed in. "Sorry for not being a gentleman," he murmured.

She chuckled. "Guess that's what happens when you live a double life."

A tiny argument sprang to his thoughts, but he dismissed it. He wouldn't ruin the day by referring to his reasons for being Justin Bellamy.

The sun shone with usual brightness but seemed to hold less bite and more kiss. The wind blew, but gently. Or so it seemed to Judd. The sky had a diamond-like brilliance as they delivered the clean laundry then headed down the dusty road toward Bowwell.

"Have you been to the town before?" Madge asked.

"No. You'll have to provide directions as to where we should eat and where the play is held."

"There's also a park in the center of town, though I wonder how it's fared with the drought and all."

"We'll have to check it out." He hoped there'd be lots of sheltered coves where he might admire her beauty and perhaps steal a kiss. Remembering how she'd reacted last time he kissed her, he decided to avoid the pleasing occupation until he could be certain she'd welcome such attention.

The hour-long drive passed quickly and pleasantly as they discussed how the Burns family was doing.

"Conrad still hasn't changed his mind about marrying Joanie?"

"No. He's a stubborn man. I'm afraid he's going to break her heart."

She shifted the discussion to Gratton. "His mother is due to arrive soon. The place is fixed up nicely for her."

He didn't want to ruin the day by talking of that man, but he couldn't resist one little question. "Are you sure the woman is his mother?"

She sucked in air nosily. "Of course she is. He showed me her picture. Who else do you think she might be?"

"I don't know. Maybe a woman he doesn't want to confess to having no legitimate relationship to."

She studied him intently. He fixed his gaze firmly on the road ahead. He should have kept his doubts to himself.

Finally, when he thought he would suffocate from trying to keep his thoughts under control and his face turned forward, she spoke. "I hope you don't let what happened to your mother make you bitter and mistrusting."

Her words sliced through his conscience. Knowing Madge's concern, he almost threw his plans out the window. Almost—but not quite. "I don't intend to let it. I have one goal in mind—see a certain man brought to justice. That's all."

She turned to watch the passing dusty fields. "I'm

looking forward to the play. Everyone says it's hilarious."

He gratefully accepted her attempt to avoid conflict between them. "I'm looking forward to it, too." Only it wasn't thoughts of the play filling him with eager anticipation. It was the pleasure of her company.

Soon they came to the main street of Bowwell. Unlike most prairie towns that had one long road running either perpendicular or at right angles to the railway tracks, the streets in this town formed a T. One corner was a square filled with poplar and maple trees with benches along the perimeter and pathways leading inward to the heart.

"That's the park I mentioned. It looks better than I expected, though there is usually an abundance of flowers in the planters."

He parked at the side of the street. "We have lots of time. Shall we wander through it?"

"I'd like that."

He rushed around and opened the door. As she stepped to the sidewalk, he held his arm out for her. She tucked her arm through his and smiled up shyly. He pulled his elbow close, pressing her hand to his ribs.

The park, although struggling against drought and grasshoppers, was still a pleasant place. Big trees sheltered Judd and Madge from view as they walked along the path. More benches were placed sporadically, inviting them to sit and talk. But they sauntered on. Only one woman hurried through, shepherding three children ahead of her. Muted sounds reached them from the busy streets, but other than that, they might have been alone.

Something nagged at his thoughts and demanded an answer. "What made you change your mind?"

Only the slight twitch of her arm at his side gave any indication that she knew what he referred to.

"About what?"

"Being in my company. I'd begun to think I carried the plague the way you avoided me."

"I didn't avoid you."

"You did." He pulled her around to face him. "Maybe someday you'll feel you can tell the truth about why."

Madge stared at a spot past his shoulder. "Because…we thought…Mother planned…" She drew in a deep breath and looked directly at him. "I'll tell you what. I'll tell you the reason when you tell the others the truth about who you are."

He searched her eyes a long time, and what he saw filled him with hope and longing. He wanted to be completely honest with her, let her see into every corner of his heart, open every thought to her. He nodded. "It's a deal, but not just yet."

Disappointment flashed across her face, and she lowered her head.

He wanted to lift her chin and kiss away every doubt, but how could he when he hid the truth from her? "You keep your secret and I'll keep mine." It should have made him feel justified, but instead, it built an invisible wall between them.

No reason to let it. He had told her all she needed to know. She would only be hurt if she learned Gratton was the man he sought to bring to justice. And whatever *her* secret, it did not stop him from caring about her and hoping there could be something special and lasting between them.

He pulled her to his side again. "Let's see the rest of the park." But too soon, they reached the end and had to retrace their steps.

They returned to the heart of town. "Where do you suggest we eat?"

She appeared to ponder the question. "I've only eaten in one place with a very special person."

Jealousy ground through his insides. He kept his voice low. "Yeah. Who?" Somehow, despite his intentions, his words sounded like gravel under the wheels of the car.

She noticed and laughed. "My father."

He chuckled, as pleased as she. "Would you like to go there?"

"Yes, I would." She still held his arm and pulled

him to the right. "It's the Silver Star dining room down at the end of the block."

He'd have let her take him anywhere, but she only led him to a low building with a row of windows facing the street, through which he saw white table-cloths, points hanging neatly from each side. They stepped inside, and a young woman in a black dress and tiny white apron led them to a table next to the window, partially hidden by a branching fern.

The girl slipped away, leaving them to study the menus. Judd didn't care what they ate, but he wanted the evening to be special, memorable for Madge.

"The beef tenderloin sounds good."

"It does."

He ordered fresh lemonade to accompany the meal and sat back to study Madge as they waited for their food. Aware of his scrutiny, she darted little glances at him and fiddled with her fork. Realizing he made her nervous, he shifted to look out the window. "Why did your father bring you here?"

She chuckled. "Because I insisted I should accompany him when he came to inspect a piece of machinery. I wanted to see him conduct business." A faraway look filled her eyes. "He was a canny businessman. He managed to walk away from most deals pleased with his negotiations while the other party took his money and considered themselves fortunate to have made such a good bargain. I learned a lot from him."

He could see her doing the same—getting the deal she wanted, yet leaving the other person thinking he had gotten what he wanted. "Your father sounds like a good man."

"He was a great man. He never compromised, yet he never accepted a bad deal, either. I miss him." She sighed. "I wonder if he would be disappointed in me for persuading Mother to let the farmland go."

Her sadness tore at Judd's insides, and he reached across the table and captured her restless hands. "If he was the astute businessman you say he was, he would know and approve that you did what you must to salvage your home."

The smile she favored him with slid through his thoughts like warm honey, sweet and healing. He held her gaze, drinking deeply of the way she openly met his look, silently baring her heart to him. "Madge, I—"

"Your meals." The interruption ended the opportunity to say how he felt.

He swallowed back the urge to tell the woman he didn't care if he ate or not. But Madge smiled her thanks.

They waited until the server moved off. Madge gave him an expectant look. He realized she waited for him to offer the blessing. For an uncomfortable moment, Judd wasn't sure what to do. He wasn't much for praying out loud in public. Yet his conscience wouldn't allow him to partake of such a lovely meal with Madge across from him without thanking God. Madge smiled sweetly and his nervousness disappeared.

"I'll say the grace," he said.

She reached for his hands and bowed her head. For a frantic heartbeat he couldn't move. Couldn't think. Her gesture was so full of simple faith in him, it made his lungs stall. He vowed he would never do anything to make her trust falter. Then he bowed his head and, from a heart overflowing with gratitude, he offered a sincere prayer of thanks.

For a few minutes, they ate in silence. The food was as good as it smelled.

She paused. "What was it like growing up with three brothers?"

He thought of Louisa, who didn't have the energy to do anything vigorous, and Sally, who was so quiet and shy she almost disappeared into the woodwork. Amusement filled him. "I expect a lot different than growing up with two sisters."

She chuckled. "I would think so. I want to know about it. Were you mischievous?"

"We were a handful. It's a wonder we didn't drive my mother crazy."

"Why? What did you do?"

He tipped his head and pretended to study her seriously. "If I tell you, you might decide you want nothing more to do with me."

Her eyes sparkled. "Maybe. Maybe not. Why not take a chance and see?"

"Okay. First, let me say that Levi managed to stay out of trouble better than the rest of us. Being the youngest by a few years, Mother managed to keep him closer to home. But the three of us—me, Carson and Redford—we ran wild. Nothing bad, of course."

"Of course not." She looked suitably doubtful. "But details, sir. I'm waiting for details."

He could not refuse the interest flashing in her eyes. "We used to tie ropes to trees and see how far we could swing from one to the other. When we were much younger, you understand."

"Of course," she murmured.

"Sounds innocent enough, but we kept getting bolder, making the distance between ropes longer. One day we made it to our greatest challenge. I was the biggest and I made it safely." He chuckled. "I really had to reach and guessed Carson, who was close in size, might make it. He did. By then we both knew Redford was too small, but we nudged each other and didn't say anything. You see, he was always insistent he could do anything we could. So we let him try."

"Tsk. How badly was he hurt?"

"Would you believe he broke both arms?"

She gasped. "He did? How awful. And to think you could have stopped him. I hope you were suitably punished."

He roared with laughter. "He didn't break anything, though we had a hard time explaining away the bruises all over his body."

She stared in disbelief. Then her eyes narrowed. "You tricked me."

He nodded, his heart brimming with amusement.

She laughed—a rich, full-throated sound. "I pity your poor mother. I expect you made her life... interesting. Challenging."

"Mother was always a good sport. She understood the difference between innocent, boyish fun and maliciousness. Beats me how she could have been sucked in by that shyster."

She sobered and looked ready to tell him again how he should leave things in God's hands.

He did not want to hear it. "We gave the teacher a heart attack one day. Carson had a pet mouse he carried around. I didn't want to be outdone by my brother, so I tamed one, too, though I have to say mice aren't easy to tame and even harder to keep in one place. We decided to take them to school one day."

Her expression flared with surprise and shock.

"Don't ask why. It seemed like a reasonable thing

at the time. We put them in our overalls." He patted his chest to indicate the breast pocket. "They both wiggled loose while we were standing saying the Lord's Prayer and ran up to the front. Mrs. Porter opened her eyes to see the little guys scurry across her feet. Boy, did she scream."

Madge shuddered. "I'm beginning to think I was fortunate to have sisters."

"Our punishment was to memorize three chapters in the Bible. And we didn't get to choose them. I can still say them. 'In the beginning was the Word, and the Word was with God—' You want to hear it all?"

Her laughter again tugged at his heart. "I'll pass." She grew more serious. "When did you become a Christian?"

"That teacher who made us memorize Bible passages?"

She nodded.

"She also told us she forgave us and went on to explain how some things aren't only silly tricks. They are sins and only God can forgive them. We'd heard it before, both at home and at church, but when Mrs. Porter told us, it made sense and both Carson and I knelt at our desks and asked Jesus to forgive us."

"That's sweet. But Jesus is so much more than a means of forgiveness."

"I know what you're going to say. Let's leave it for now."

"I just wish you would see how God can be trusted to take care of justice."

"As the oldest son, I have a duty to protect my mother."

Her eyes grew dark and troubled, but she only shook her head.

Knowing one sure way to divert her from the topic that created dissent between them, he said, "Tell me how you became a Christian."

"My father taught us well about God's love and care. He always came to our rooms and said our evening prayers. One night he simply asked if I had yet decided to be part of God's family. I said I'd like to be."

"You did it to please your father?"

"In part, but I truly believed the things I had learned and I was ready. He did the same for Louisa and Sally. We could never figure out how he knew when each of us was ready."

"Sounds like he knew his girls. Just like Mother knew her boys. You know, we could never fool her. She always was aware of when we'd done something we shouldn't have."

"What about your father? You never speak of him."

"He died when I was young—shortly after Levi was born. I can barely remember him. Mostly I remember being the man of the family, making sure

Mother and the younger boys were taken care of."
He'd failed in his responsibilities more than once, but
never to the degree he had in letting Gratton steal
Mother's home.

Madge watched him closely, and he realized
his regret and bitterness likely showed on his face.
He didn't want to hear any more about letting God
manage without his help.

"I believe it's time to go to the play." He paid the
bill, and they left the restaurant.

"It's in the town hall." Again she rested her hand
in the crook of his elbow.

Again, he pressed her arm close.

"Thank you for the lovely meal and for telling me
more about yourself."

"You're welcome. I enjoyed learning more about
you, too." He would never get tired of listening to
her, hearing of her childhood. He would never get
tired of her company. Perhaps today was the start of
them becoming more than mere friends.

Chapter Ten

Madge made no objection when Judd pressed her arm to his side. Why would she? She loved it. She wanted this evening to last forever. Too soon she'd have to return home to reality, to face Mother's faintly chiding glance and Louisa's...only, something about her sister had changed. Maybe putting aside self-pity, as she'd confessed, had made her more generous. She'd shown unusual kindness by seeing Madge got her chores done in time to attend the play. But it seemed more than that. Why hadn't she protested when Madge had said she and Justin were going to the play? Was she that certain of his interest? Or was she pretending a generosity she didn't feel? But she'd never known Louisa to be deceitful, so she had to believe her actions were genuinely kind. But what did it mean?

Determined not to deal with it before she had to,

she pushed the questions aside. For now she would accept the pleasure of the evening and face the consequences when she must.

She enjoyed her time with Judd, seeing him as a man who wanted to protect his loved ones. The idea thrilled her to the core. Yet she feared for him. Feared his path would lead him into danger. At the very least, would cause him to disobey God. But she had said all she could. She'd pressed him to trust God. She must do the same in this situation.

A crowd gathered at the hall doorway, everyone jostling good-naturedly to be admitted first. Judd dropped his arm across her shoulders and pulled her close to shield her from some young man who got a little too enthusiastic with his pushing.

Her heart swelled with pleasure at his gesture. She breathed deeply of his scent. A warm sense of well being filled her limbs with a delightful melting sensation.

They edged into the hall, paused at the ticket booth to purchase admission, and then he led her down the aisle to a place where they would see and hear well.

They settled in, and he reached for her hand, pulled it back into the bend of his arm, then rested his palm over her fingers.

She ducked her head to hide the pleasure she suspected would be all too evident in her face. Tried to tell herself it was only because he felt responsible to protect those under his care.

He leaned close to whisper, "I haven't offended you, have I?"

Swallowing back a strange tightness in her throat, she looked into his dark eyes, not inches away. He seemed uncertain, and she suddenly cared not if he saw how much she enjoyed this closeness, but her voice refused to work. She could only shake her head.

"Good." With a wide grin he settled back, though she didn't miss the fact that he leaned closer.

The lights dimmed and the play began. It was funny and touching. The audience laughed and clapped and cheered. For Madge, the magic was multiplied each time she glanced at Judd and met his eyes, sharing the moment with him. More than once, their eyes locked, and for an instant they were alone in the room, unaware of the others, their interest in the entertainment forgotten.

Thankfully, the audience would make a noise reminding her they were not alone, forcing her to turn and concentrate on the activity on the stage.

It ended to a standing ovation and several curtain calls.

Judd stepped into the aisle and waited for her to move in front of him. Everyone pushed toward the exit. He cupped her shoulder with his big, warm hand and guided her toward the door. She was protected, sheltered by his body.

She would have gladly stood in the crowd forever, pressed to him, guarded by him. But all too soon they broke into fresh air. With no more excuse to stand so close, Madge moved a step away.

Judd caught her hand and pulled her to his side. Their pathway led them past the park, and at his suggestion she gladly accompanied him down the shadowed lanes.

"Did you enjoy the play?" he murmured.

"It was fun." She'd enjoyed his company even more.

"I sure laughed when they went to the garden and he tried to tell her he still loved her, but when he sat on the wheelbarrow it broke."

Everyone had laughed. "They seemed to be plagued with nothing but disasters."

"Yet they did manage to admit their love."

"But one thing bothers me. Why did they waste so many years?" The main characters had been childhood sweethearts, but the man had wandered away and married another. The play took place seventeen years later when he returned, after his wife died, to find the leading lady an old maid owner of a huge ranch. "Besides, didn't it look like he had suddenly found out she had this big ranch? As if he was interested in her riches." As soon as she spoke the words, she wished she could pull them back. The last thing she wanted was to remind him of his mother and his quest to see the gold digger man brought to justice. Quickly she rushed on before he realized what she'd said. "I know if I loved someone, I would tell them. I wouldn't want to waste seventeen years."

He reached for her hand and squeezed it. "Me, neither." Then he stopped and pulled her into his arms, looking down into her face.

Her heart rapped so hard, she was sure he would feel it.

"In fact, it's time I said I think I might be falling in love with you."

"But…" *You are supposed to fall in love with Louisa.* Madge had done all she could to stay out of the way so it would happen. Hadn't she? What would Mother say? Louisa?

But the arguments fell to the ground like last year's leaves.

She had just vowed she would tell someone if she loved them, but her mouth refused to work. All she could do was bury her face against his chest, smiling as she felt his heartbeat beneath her cheek.

He seemed to understand her unspoken message and wrapped her more tightly to him, their hearts beating as one. Then he shifted and caught her chin with his strong fingers, tipping her face upward.

Even in the dim light, she saw the eager question

in his eyes. For answer she stood on tiptoe and lifted her head. He read her intention and quickly claimed her lips. This time she had nothing to fear, nothing to hide, nothing to hold her back, and she put her whole heart and all her love into the kiss. He gave equally as much back, carrying her upward on the wings of love and joy.

He broke away with a sigh. "I think we better go home."

She snuggled to his side. She was in no hurry, but Mother would worry if they were too late. She hated the thought of facing Mother, though, so she clung to his arm and pressed her cheek to his shoulder as they returned to the car.

He held his door open and retained hold of her hand as she slipped in, preventing her from sliding across the seat to the window. He started the car and negotiated his way out of town, then used only one hand to drive—the other pulling Madge closer.

She didn't object in the least. A whole hour together to enjoy his company. She let her head rest on his shoulder.

Their conversation often fell silent on the drive. She was content simply to be with him. He hadn't exactly said he loved her, but she knew he meant it. She didn't understand her hesitation to confess her love, then smiled as she recalled something her father had said. "Never tell a man right off you love him. Wait until he commits himself." His advice made her decide to wait. Once spoken, the words became a vow.

When he started talking about how he'd like to buy the Cotton place and fix it up, she knew it was only a matter of time until Judd would make the commitment.

He gave a mocking laugh. "'Course, I could never afford to buy it from the bank."

Madge said nothing. Many young couples were putting off marriage because of financial difficulties. She did not want to be another. All she could do was ask God to provide a way for their love to thrive and come to completion in marriage.

She chuckled. Here she was thinking marriage, and he had only said he might be falling in love. It was because she had already fallen solidly, irrevocably in love. It was such a sweet, overpowering feeling it couldn't be dimmed, even by the idea of facing Mother and confessing her feelings.

"What's so funny?"

"Nothing. It's just been a great night. I will never forget it."

His arm tightened around her. "Me, neither."

All too soon they arrived at home. The yard lay in darkness, allowing him to step out and pull her after him without fear of anyone seeing him as Judd.

He leaned his hands against the car, one arm

on either side of her, preventing her from hurrying away, though she had no intention of doing so.

She would gladly remain here sheltered by his arms, feeling his breath on her cheek, loving him so much it made her shiver.

He lowered his head.

She met him halfway, clutching at his shirtfront. He kissed her thoroughly. After a satisfying moment, he lifted his head, breaking the contact. She sucked in air.

"Thank you for a nice evening." His voice was thick, and she buried the sweetness of the sound in her heart.

"You're welcome."

He kissed her again, quickly, then backed away. "Good night."

She hesitated. But he was right. Time to head indoors. She brushed his chin lightly, delighting in the feel of his thick beard that had tickled her as they'd kissed. What would his face feel like shaven? She recalled a strong jaw and chiseled chin from their first encounter. Remembering that incident, she chuckled.

"What's amusing you now?"

"I was remembering how I almost bowled you off your feet the first time I saw you."

He cupped her head between his palms. "You certainly left an unforgettable impression. Now go to bed."

With a smile on her face and a song in her heart, she crossed the yard. And came to a decision. She would keep her love a secret from the others for now. Until Judd revealed his true identity and Mother realized there was no Justin for Louisa to marry.

Madge's work seemed lighter over the next few days. She sang as she hung sheets, and she ran up the stairs as if the baskets she carried were empty. Every time she passed the living room, Judd glanced up and smiled at her.

She tried to be restrained, for she didn't want Mother or her sisters to notice. But they must have wondered when they looked outside and observed her staring into space, a smile on her lips and her work forgotten.

Today was her afternoon to work at Gratton's. His mother was due to arrive, and George had asked her to come by and help her settle in.

Alone in the car with no one to hear and wonder, she sang. If this was how being in love felt, they ought to capture the feeling and sell it to sick people, who would recover instantly and begin dancing.

She laughed at her silliness and sobered as she parked in front of the Gratton house. She looked forward to meeting Mrs. Gratton.

She smoothed her hair as best she could, stepped

out and brushed her skirt, then marched to the house and knocked.

"Come in," a gentle voice called.

She stepped inside. A silver-haired woman she recognized from George's picture sat in a high-backed chair watching the door as if she'd been there for hours.

"You must be Madge. I've been waiting for you. I'm George's mother. I suppose you think you should call me Mrs. Gratton, but I don't want you to. I much prefer my given name, so call me Grace."

Madge giggled. George was right. His mother's body might be somewhat frail, but her spirit was obviously not.

"George made me promise on the Bible—really. On the Bible, if you can imagine. As if he couldn't trust his own mother's word any other way. What a naughty child. I should have spanked him more when he was young." Her twinkling eyes informed Madge she thought nothing of the sort. "Oh, yes. I started to say he made me promise not to unpack a thing but to wait for you. So here you are, and now we can unpack." She pushed to her feet a little slowly, as if her joints hurt, but she picked up pace as she headed for her bedroom.

"He fixed up this room downstairs. When I asked what was wrong with the bedrooms upstairs, the impudent boy said nothing except they were upstairs, and I wasn't to set so much as one foot on the steps. Can you imagine him thinking he could boss me around like that?" She turned, caught the way Madge grinned and smiled back. "I let him think he can so he feels better."

The woman was amazing. She kept up an amusing prattle while she perched on the edge of the bed—in obedience to George's orders, she said—and supervised Madge unpacking her stuff.

Two hours later, Grace declared she was satisfied with the work. "Now we must have tea. You'll make it, of course."

"Certainly." She enjoyed Grace's company. They laughed together over tea, and then Grace kept her amused as Madge prepared supper for them.

"Would you stay and eat with us?" Grace asked.

There was a time she would have welcomed the invitation, but now she couldn't wait to get home and see Judd and share the news of what a delightful woman Grace Gratton was. The others would love hearing of her spark as much as Madge had enjoyed it. She'd get double the pleasure—the firsthand experience and the joy of sharing it with the family and seeing their spirits lift.

Over the following days, Madge and Judd managed to steal some time together every evening. Sometimes it was to deliver laundry. Other times it was to simply sit outside in the shade and talk, usually with Mother or one of her sisters joining them, but occasionally they were left alone. Madge wondered that Louisa didn't spend every minute possible with them, but she cherished those times alone too much to beg trouble, so she didn't say anything.

She'd discovered Judd was a great storyteller and a tease. As he recounted tales from his time working as a cowboy, she laughed. But she learned something more. Once Judd set his mind on some action, he didn't let it go, whether it was riding a horse, bringing a cow in or…bringing to justice the man he blamed for his mother's financial difficulties. Although the trait was admirable, she couldn't help but worry how his plan would end. And she prayed he would find peace. Yet when she questioned him, he said he still sought the man.

"Perhaps he isn't here." She hoped Judd was mistaken and would drop his quest.

"No. He's here. I just have to watch." He would say no more.

Judd also asked about her childhood and her work. His interest made her open up and share things she had almost forgotten—dreams, hopes, failures, disappointments.…

She had never felt so safe with anyone before.

The afternoons she worked at Gratton's were enjoyable, even though they meant she would not see Judd again until after supper.

Her mind drifted from the meal she was preparing for the Grattons, and she stared out the window. She heard the door open as George came in. Grace had gone to her bedroom to rest, and he paused to look in on her.

Madge sighed and pulled her mind back to her task. But just as she started to turn from the window, a movement caught her eye. A man clung to the boards of the fence across the lane. She squinted. It was Judd. Her heart danced for joy. He'd come to wait for her. She hurried through the rest of her work and refused Grace's invitation to join them.

Outside she waited at her car, but Judd did not appear.

How odd. She delayed her departure until she knew it was useless to linger.

Had she been mistaken? Or had he rushed home to wait for her there?

Her heart bubbled with joy, and she hurried down the road. The family had moved suppertime back so she could eat with them. Mother and the girls sat at the table as she stepped into the room. But Judd was absent. Where was he? If he hadn't waited for her in town, why wasn't he here?

Mother provided the information. "Justin said he had things to attend to and wouldn't be here." A trickle of suspicion crowded the corners of her mind. What was he doing watching the Gratton place? That would make George…no! It couldn't be George. Perhaps Judd only hoped for a chance to speak to her.

Madge gave her attention to the food and hoped no one would notice her confusion.

The next day, Judd didn't mention his absence the evening before, and she would not. It was enough to have him at her side, enjoying the quiet of the evening. Yet he said good-night early, and later, she thought she detected him leaving the soddie. No doubt off to find the man he sought. Again, the uneasy suspicion. Was he watching the Grattons?

It wasn't possible.

Two days later, she put the finishing touches on supper for Grace and George. Again she stared out the window, and as George came home, she saw Judd lingering in the shadows.

He watched the house. No doubt about it.

Horror filled her thoughts. It made cruel sense. The questions he asked, his interest in what she did at the Gratton house.

Her insides sucked flat as she realized why he was so keen to spend time with her. A cry filled her lungs and remained there, trapped by the awful truth.

"I have to go," she murmured to Grace and George. They must have wondered at her hasty retreat and the fact that she raced out the back door instead of leaving from the front as she always did.

Judd jerked away from the shadows as she dashed into the yard. He looked about, as if hoping for escape, and then tucked in his chin and spun on his heel.

"Judd, wait!" She would not let him leave without an explanation.

He stopped. She didn't slow her steps until she stood close enough to see the way his eyelids flickered. Breathing hard, as much from the way her insides twisted as from exertion, she faced him. She knew her expression likely revealed something of what she felt—hurt, anger and a thousand things that defied explanation.

"Why are you watching this house?"

"'Spect you've figured it out already."

"You're wrong. George is not a bad man like you think."

He crossed his arms over his chest and looked unimpressed. "If he were obviously evil, he wouldn't be fooling helpless women, would he?"

"You're wrong," she repeated. "But too stubborn to admit it."

"I'd be glad to admit it if I thought it was true."

She leaned back, almost drowning in a confusion of protests and realizations. "You used me to spy on them."

"How do you get that?"

"Maybe everything you said was only to make it easy for you to get information on them." Anger built like a balloon, ready to burst. "Was that all I was? A way to find out about the Grattons?" The truth of her words burned away her anger. Left her empty. So empty all she could hear was the echo of her silent screaming pain. "From now on you'll have to do your own dirty work." She spun around and marched to her car.

"Madge, you know that's not true. My feelings for you have nothing to do with the Grattons." He grabbed her arm to force her to stop and listen.

She jerked back. "Your behavior is despicable. How can I believe anything you say?"

His hand fell off and he let her go.

She stifled a cry as she hurried away. Thankfully she had heeded Father's advice and refrained from telling Judd she loved him. But it didn't change the fact that she did.

She'd loved foolishly and too eagerly.

Her hand shook as she started the car and drove homeward. How would she put him from her mind? Especially as he would be in the house tutoring Louisa.

She considered speaking to Mother, but why should anyone else pay for Madge's stupidity?

By the time she reached home, she had come to

a decision. She would avoid Judd at all costs and somehow convince her family nothing had happened. Keep busy. Work. That would be her excuse.

Stubbornness had its value, but it could not erase the pain claiming every cell of her body and catching at every breath.

Chapter Eleven

Somehow Madge managed to drive home without crashing into anything or hitting the ditch, though her mind had not been on handling the car. She parked by habit and stumbled to her room without anyone questioning her.

Numb from head to toe, she lay on her bed, pulled Macat into her arms and stared at the ceiling. How could she have been so easily fooled? Anger burned through her. Judd's actions were every bit as despicable as those he accused George of—deceiving a woman for his own gain. And he was wrong about George. She knew he was. But then, maybe she was a simpleton when it came to detecting falseness in men. Seems her trust of Judd proved that well enough.

How was she going to see him day after day? It

wasn't like she could walk away. Without her efforts, the family would lose their home.

Oh, God, what am I going to do?

But God did not send an answer.

She sat up and pushed the cat to one side. God didn't do for a person what they could do for themselves. Comfort and guidance were to be found where she always found them—in God's word. She pulled her Bible close and read page after page, seeking solace and something more—a way to cope.

Someone came to the house. She recognized Judd's voice as he spoke to Mother. Despite herself and all her resolve, her heart lurched against her chest like Mouse at the door when he heard Louisa on the other side.

Her feet hit the floor before she realized how foolish it would be to give him another chance, knowing he'd used her to get information on George.

She sank down on the bed, caught Macat in her arms again and buried her face in the warm fur. At least animals were loyal and true. They didn't pretend one thing while planning another. They simply loved you and let you love them back.

The voices stopped murmuring and the door closed. She tiptoed to the window and peeked out to see Justin limp across to the soddie and duck inside. Justin indeed! Everything about him was false—

from his name to his limp to his reasons for pretending interest in her.

He didn't so much as look over his shoulder to see if she might be at the window.

She knew her annoyance at his failure to do so made no sense, but it robbed her of the last faint hope that he truly might care.

Louisa came up and went to her room. Sally followed. She listened to the girls preparing for bed, heard Mother making rounds to check the house before she retired to her room. Then all was quiet.

All except Madge's mind. It refused to rest.

She scolded herself for being a fool. A moment later she congratulated herself for never telling him she loved him, though—her cheeks burned at the thought—she'd certainly been free enough with cuddles and kisses. Then sorrow, pain and despair filled her. How would she manage?

Only with God's help. Trusting Him had never been so challenging. Or so necessary.

She fell asleep praying.

Groggy, she stirred as she heard a car motor in the yard. Then she sighed, rolled over and fell back into a deep slumber.

Sally shook her awake. "Madge, wake up."

She struggled from a troubled sleep. There was some reason she must speak to Judd, something she had to say, but he kept dancing in and out of reach, leaving her frantic. It took her a moment to realize her thoughts were but a dream and Sally stood over her talking.

"Are you okay? You don't ever sleep in like this, especially when you have so much laundry. I've filled the tubs but…"

"What time is it?"

"It's gone past seven."

Madge leaped from the bed. "You should have wakened me before." She hurried into her work clothes and raced down the stairs and outside to start the laundry. She'd never get it all done today.

Sally followed. "We haven't had breakfast yet. We waited for you."

She would have refused, but she couldn't stop eating in order to avoid Judd. Girding a protective shell around her, she marched indoors.

The table was set for four.

Mother noticed her interest. "Justin told me last night he had family things to attend to and wouldn't be returning."

Relief scoured through her insides, followed by painful regret. Would she never see him again?

She held her chin high, determined not to reveal any hint of her pain and confusion.

Somehow she ate, did the laundry, packed heavy baskets up and down the stairs. The work was endless. She barely finished in time for supper, then had to make the deliveries.

In town, she passed the Gratton place, slowing to a crawl and checking out the back lane where she'd seen Judd.

She didn't see him. She didn't care. She never wanted to see him again. And if he hurt Grace or George…

But the pain clawing at her insides could not be denied.

The next day she was due to work at the Grattons'. Grace noted her mood immediately.

"Why the sad countenance? Some man done you wrong?"

Grace's touch of resignation made Madge smile for the first time since she'd discovered Judd's deceit. "Why must it be a man?"

"Because you are a woman. And until today the trials of the current situation in the country have not bothered you. I'm not so old I don't remember what it was like to be young and in love. Why, I fell in love with George's father when I was fourteen. Even told him so. He laughed and said I was too young to know what I was talking about." She sniffed. "Little did he know that I intended to marry him one day. And I did. He didn't stand a chance from the beginning."

Madge's smile widened. Grace would never take

no for an answer, although she might let a person think she had.

"My advice is, if you love a man and he's worthy of it, hang on and pray for him to turn around."

Madge sobered. She didn't know if Judd was worthy of her love. Through her mind ran flashes of the times they had spent together—the trip to Bowwell, the evenings they'd sat and discussed things close to their hearts. She'd felt so connected. Felt his heart to be true and honest. Even in his disguise as Justin, he'd been candid with her.

Except for the fact he intended to get even with George. It was not something she could overlook.

Grace watched her. "Ah. You have doubts. Then, my dear, listen to your head, but don't ignore your heart. Things are not always as they seem."

Though she tried, Madge couldn't see how to excuse Judd. She turned her attention to her work, glancing out the window many times but not seeing Judd. She denied any disappointment. Why would she want to see him out there spying? What would she do if she did? She certainly couldn't allow him to continue to spy on her friends.

Feeling as if she had worked three days without sleep, she made her way home and dragged herself upstairs to her room as soon as she could escape without raising questions.

Macat lay on the bed, and Madge curled around the warm body and fell asleep.

She dreamed of laundry. Piles and piles of it. The more she washed, the higher it grew until it blocked the sun. Her heart filled with wrenching terror, and she fought her way through the stacks, fighting against sheets wrapping about her. Finally she broke through to where the house stood. Only it was gone. In its place fluttered a piece of paper with the bank's name in large black letters.

She bolted upright. The mortgage payment was due at the end of the week. Thinking about Judd had pushed the thought to the back of her mind.

The panicked feeling of the dream clung to her. She sucked in air in a vain attempt to calm herself, with reminders the mortgage payment would be ready on time. She had only to wait for George to pay her.

The fear and restlessness of her dream would not leave. She got to her feet and walked to the window to stare at the dark soddie. Judd was gone. She missed him with an ache as big as the piles of laundry in her nightmare.

But did she miss Judd or the man he pretended to be—the man she wanted him to be?

Judd dusted off one of the chairs and pulled it toward the table. He'd tried camping outside, but the wind blew his stuff around. The dust invaded everything, including his eyes and his food, and he couldn't start a fire for fear of it racing away.

So he'd moved into the Cotton house, sure no one would object to him parking there for a while.

He sank his elbows to the table. He missed Madge. Had no one to blame but himself that she'd discovered his secret. Maybe he'd even wanted her to. He sure didn't like hiding the truth from her. Plus, he wanted her to be wary around George. Any man who would steal from a helpless woman needed to be watched.

But she hadn't understood. Had not tried to see the situation from his side. He couldn't face her day in, day out and pretend his heart hadn't shattered at her reaction. Besides, it was time to get on with the task bringing him here—stopping George Gratton, seeing he got his just deserts.

He dug into the beans he'd warmed at the stove. He'd walked around the farm several times and poked through every room in the house. With every step, he saw more and more possibilities for the place.

If Madge would ever forgive him… Perhaps once she understood George truly was a despicable man, she might.

He scraped the plate clean, pushed it away and hurried to town, crossing the dusty fields in swift strides. No more reason to pretend to be Justin, except he had no desire for George to learn his true identity. Not until he could discover what the man was up to in Golden Prairie. But he assured himself anyone seeing him would dismiss him as one of many homeless men who wandered the countryside.

He moseyed along the tracks as if he had nothing in mind but the next train, then angled toward the Gratton house in a circuitous route.

He knew what time George got home from work. He knew when George's mother went to bed. So far he'd been unable to spot any unusual movement around the place after that, but then he'd spent far too much time waiting for Madge and paying scant attention to other activity around the house.

All that was about to change. He would watch continually until he learned what was going on.

The first night, he went back to the Cotton place after he was certain George had retired to bed, thinking perhaps that was part of the ruse. Maybe he only wanted people to think he'd gone to bed.

So the next night he stayed until George left for work in the morning. Exhausted, he made his way back to the farm and threw himself on a cot and slept for eight hours without stirring.

Five nights in a row it was the same. The only break from the monotonous routine was Madge's arrival. Those days, he wandered down the lane to the back of the Gratton house earlier, telling himself he only wanted to be sure Madge was safe.

He caught glimpses of her through the window and as she stepped outside to sweep the step. He backed away, determined to stay out of sight, though his heart begged otherwise. If only he could make his presence known and think she would welcome him. But it wasn't possible with his task still ahead of him. He could not abandon it. Not with a clear conscience.

He stayed out of sight until she returned indoors, then relaxed marginally and continued his vigil.

George arrived home. Judd watched Madge serve the meal, then leave.

Though his heart followed after her, he forced himself to stay hidden—waiting, watching, sure that eventually he would learn what he needed.

Two nights later, his vigil was rewarded. After Mrs. Gratton retired to her room and turned out the light, a man entered by way of the front door. Judd, at the back, couldn't make out who it was, so he slipped closer until he could get a wider view through the windows. The visitor turned.

Judd saw him clearly. He stared a moment and then retreated out of sight.

The pastor.

What dealings did a man of God have with a

scoundrel like Gratton? Could he be involved in a scheme?

This situation might be more complicated than he anticipated.

Madge slowed at the turn off for the Cotton farm. She eased to the side of the road and looked at the tracks in the dust. The last two times she'd passed, she'd thought she'd seen something that shouldn't have been there. Faint depressions in the dirt, grass bent as if tramped on. Now she knew she hadn't been mistaken. Someone was going in and out of the place. She sat back and stared out the window, her hands gripping the steering wheel hard. Who could it be, and what business did they have there? She hadn't heard it had sold, and news of such would have traveled like wildfire through the town's gossip chain.

It could be harmless. Some hobos looking for shelter. Likely nothing to be concerned about.

But still, someone should investigate.

She contemplated her options. The lane was right there before her. If she was careful…

She turned the car and, with as much stealth as a banging motor allowed, headed toward the buildings.

The sunlight caught on something metallic. She found the cause and gasped. Judd's car was parked against the barn, as far out of sight as possible.

Her heart jumped with joy. He hadn't left.

Sanity pushed doubts into her thoughts, cooled her heart. There was only one reason he would still be here. To get to George.

She glanced about. Saw no sign of him. No doubt he was in town watching the Gratton house. Anger twisted through her. Anger at his duplicity, the fact he would stay for revenge but not for her.

There was only one way she could imagine putting an end to this plan of his.

Madge prepared tea for Grace—beautiful teacups with matching teapot, creamer and sugar dish. "I lost most of my nice things when the financial markets took a hit," she had several times explained. "George blames himself. As if he had the power to control the ups and downs of business. I told him we let greed get us into this situation, and now we have no one to blame but our own greedy natures. Why, I think God must look down from heaven and wonder if He didn't make a mistake in giving us free will. It's not like we've used it especially wisely, is it? Why, when I think of the Great War…" She shuddered. "If I could, I would march all the naughty boys— and it's always men who start wars, isn't it? I would march them—oh, I don't know where." She pressed her fingertips together and considered the problem.

Madge smiled. She liked the way Grace's conversations dashed from one thing to another, often finishing the first thought down a long convoluted conversation trail.

Grace dropped her fingers and beamed. "I know what I'd do with them. I'd give them all the orphaned babies in the world to look after. Why, by the time they changed all the nappies, washed all the little garments, fed the poor little ones and cleaned the house, they would be much too tired to think of going to war."

Madge chuckled at the solution. "Too bad they don't think to let women rule the world."

Grace sighed delicately. "But God is ultimately in control. I know He can do a better job than I, even if I don't understand why He lets things go on in such a shameful way. I guess if I've learned one fact in my long life—" She added a dramatic sigh for good measure. "It's that things have a way of working out in ways that surprise us. I cling to a verse in Romans, 'And we know that all things work together for good to them that love God, to them who are called according to His purpose.' Chapter eight—one of my favorite chapters. I recall memorizing it in school."

Madge wondered if it was one of the chapters Judd had memorized for his teacher. Her glance went to the window. Was he out there? She filled the fine teapot and set out some sugar cookies she'd made.

Grace presided over the table with a regal bearing. "I used to have ladies drop in at teatime."

"You will again, once you get to know a few. The ladies will be thrilled to visit with you." Tea was a great time to entertain guests, and Madge knew exactly who Grace should entertain—Judd Kirk.

She had to be patient. Two days ago she'd been certain she'd seen his shadow lean out from the protection of the shed in the backyard. Today she was ready. "Excuse me a moment."

She slipped out the front door and edged around the side of the house, knowing if Judd was leaning against the wall, she could approach from his blind side. Quietly, she moved along. As she neared the last corner, she paused, caught her breath and listened.

Did she hear him breathing?

Certain she did, she gathered up her muscles and burst around the corner. He was there, and she grabbed his arm. "I thought I might find you here."

She feared he would try to escape at her touch, but once he saw who it was, he settled back. "What are you doing?"

"I think it's time you came out of hiding."

"Are you crazy?" He tried to shake her off, but she held on tightly, causing him to stare at her hand as if checking that it truly belonged to her. "You promised you wouldn't give away my true identity."

"I did. Of course, at the time I didn't realize you

were set on dishing out vengeance to people I happen to care for."

He grabbed her shoulder. "You can't take back your word."

"I don't intend to." She hoped and prayed he would do so himself. "I keep hoping you'll admit you are mistaken about George."

"When will you accept I'm not?" His eyes bored into her, pleading with her to agree with him.

She saw his longing. Suspected her expression conveyed the emptiness and loneliness she'd experienced since he'd left. "Judd." Her voice fell to a pleading whisper. "Give it up."

A shadow crossed his face, and anything she thought she'd seen disappeared in hardness. "I can't."

She pushed aside the emotions clogging her thoughts—how she missed him, wanted him—and returned to her original plan. "I was afraid you'd be stubborn. So I'm inviting you to tea." She pulled her arm through his elbow, firmly leading him up the sidewalk.

"Tea?" Poor man sounded bemused and suspicious at the same time.

She'd counted on a measure of surprise to give her a moment's advantage. They made it three feet before he realized she led him toward the back door of the Gratton house.

He stopped. "I'm not going in there."

She urged him forward a step. "Why not? You might discover something to your advantage."

He dug in his heels.

"Unless you're afraid of a sweet little old lady."

"Of course I'm not." He allowed her to steer him ahead, then stopped again. "You must promise you won't tell my real name."

"Justin Bellamy it is. For now."

Without further urging, although she kept a firm hold on his arm just in case, he walked toward the door.

"Grace," Madge called. "I've brought company for tea." She led Judd into the dining room.

Grace looked up and smiled gently, though her eyes twinkled. "Why, where did you find this fine gentleman?"

Madge jabbed her elbow into Judd's side to make sure he understood the irony of Grace's words. "He was outside. Grace, allow me to introduce Justin Bellamy. He's my sister Louisa's tutor. Well versed in Greek and the arts, I understand."

Judd nudged her in the ribs to warn her not to get carried away.

Grace waved to a chair. "How nice to have a gentleman join us for tea. Bellamy, you say? I knew some Bellamys back in Toronto. Geoffrey and Janet Bellamy. Any relation of yours?"

Judd sank to the chair. "I don't think so, ma'am."

Grace poured tea and handed out sugar and cream. She passed the cookies. "Madge made these for me. They're delicious. But then, everything Madge does, she does well. I suppose you know that already, young man."

Madge groaned. But Judd grinned. "From what I've seen, she's a veritable dynamo."

Madge spared him a glower before she turned to Grace. "He's not interested in my—"

"Graces?" Grace provided. "I've always enjoyed using that word. I find it hard to believe the man isn't interested, unless his eyesight is faltering." She fixed Judd with an innocent pair of eyes that Madge knew were hiding a spark of mischief fit to start a raging fire. "How about it, Mr. Bellamy? Do you have something wrong with your eyes?"

"Not a thing, ma'am."

He sounded far too pleased for Madge's peace of mind. She prayed God would use this opportunity to show Judd that Grace was a sweet lady, adored and spoiled by her son. Then he'd realize George could not possibly hurt anyone, especially a woman.

"Now tell me where you got your expertise in Greek and the arts."

The two of them were soon sparring good-naturedly about the virtues of one university over another and which artists could be considered worthy.

They disagreed vigorously about which artists were the best and why.

"I used to have an original by a fairly modern painter who is gaining a bit of renown," Grace said. "I lost it, along with most of my treasures. As I told Madge, greed caused our misfortune. I have regrets over losing most of my beautiful things, but now I see how God is working it out for my good. I have this lovely young woman to keep me company several days a week, and now I've met a gentleman with a sharp mind, if rather questionable taste when it comes to the great artists." She laughed.

Judd pushed his chair back. "I really must be leaving."

Madge watched harshness cross his expression, followed swiftly by a genuine grin.

"It's been a delight meeting you and trying to convince you of your error in artistic choices."

Grace chuckled. "It's been my pleasure. See the young man out, Madge."

"Of course." She led the way out of the room.

"No need to hurry back," Grace called.

Madge's cheeks grew uncomfortably warm.

Judd laughed and murmured, "She appreciates me."

Madge opened the door. "She doesn't know the truth, does she? What would she think if she knew you were trying to destroy her son?"

Judd's jaw clenched. "By the sounds of it, he's gambled away her things, too. She might just thank me."

"You know she wouldn't. Think about what you plan. Think about Grace and what your actions would do to her."

Judd walked from the house with long strides. Not once did he glance back at her.

Chapter Twelve

As Judd walked away, he realized he should never have allowed Madge to force him into the house. But he'd been so startled by her appearance and her touch, he'd been too befuddled to refuse.

"Shoot," he muttered to the wind. No matter what he did, where he went, he could not get her out of his mind. He snorted. More like he couldn't get her from under his skin. His frustration stirred anger in his soul. What right did she have to sneak up and scare the liver from him? For a moment he'd wondered if his thoughts had led to her turning up. It was downright scary.

He curled his fists and mentally banged them against his forehead. He reached the rail tracks before he realized how far he'd gone and ground to a halt.

This was not where he should be. No, George

would be home shortly, and he needed to watch the man.

What was the pastor doing visiting him? Certainly he might be there for spiritual guidance, but Judd simply couldn't accept that possibility. Not without proof. He knew what George had done to his mother. Feared it would happen again, though he'd yet to find evidence. But working in the bank gave George opportunity to learn people's finances, learn the value of different properties. It was only a matter of time until Gratton picked a mark.

When he did, Judd intended to be ready.

He sank in the dusty yellow grass and wrapped his arms about his knees, pulling them to his chest as if he could protect himself from the war of emotions raging through him.

Calm down. Think rationally.

Someone had to stop George. Bring him to justice. That was Judd's chosen task and solemn responsibility.

But whatever he did to George would directly affect Grace, and he'd liked the woman. No doubt, exactly Madge's intention.

George had to pay. But making him pay would hurt a sweet innocent lady. Just as George had hurt Judd's mother.

Would Judd's actions be any more or less despicable than George's in the end?

He pressed his face to his knees. *God in heaven, I don't know what to do.* Could he trust God to take care of providing justice? He hadn't seen any evidence of it. Could he hope to regain what his mother had lost? Only, he admitted, if he could either get Gratton to admit he had the money squirreled away somewhere or could intimidate him into offering some kind of compensation. It was the best he could hope for. Yet the idea didn't sit as comfortably with him as he'd pretended in front of Madge. After meeting Grace, the whole thing made him feel a bit of a bully.

But what else could he do?

He stared out at the drifting soil, driven endlessly by the wind. The sun shone with unrelenting heat. The sky was brittle. Too bright for his eyes, and he squinted.

How could he trust God when things were so bad? It was more than George. It was the economy, the weather, everything.

Surely if God was loving and fair, He would put an end to this.

Bits and pieces of scripture he had memorized so long ago blasted through his mind, as if driven by the wind: 'The world was made by Him and the world knew Him not.' 'Every branch that beareth not fruit, He taketh away; and every branch that beareth fruit, He purgeth it, that it may bring forth more fruit.'

Could it be all this hardship had an eternal purpose? Was an eternal purpose enough reason for suffering? Could he wait until eternity to see his mother's suffering addressed?

It simply didn't feel right.

He bolted to his feet and strode back the way he had come. But halfway there, he changed his mind and headed for the Cotton place.

Madge watched for Judd to return, but when it was time to leave she'd seen no further sign of him. Had he changed his mind? She prayed meeting Grace had convinced him to do so.

Yet her thoughts troubled her as she drove down the road. She wouldn't be satisfied until she heard from Judd's own lips that he'd dropped the whole idea of revenge.

She slowed as she passed the Cotton place. If he was there, she could speak to him.

Her face warmed at the conversation that had followed his departure. Grace was convinced Judd was the man of Madge's choice and had sung his praises.

Not that Madge needed to hear them. She needed no convincing. But he was living a double life, and he planned something that would hurt Grace and George.

"Life is not always as easy as one, two, three,"

she'd murmured in protest of Grace's continued chatter.

At the sadness in her eyes, Madge wished she'd kept silent.

"My dear," the older woman had said. "Life will always be complicated. But we must not let it steal the sweetness waiting for us every day. Even when everything seems dark and forbidding, God is there offering light."

Madge nodded. "I know that." But she found it harder to believe and trust than she had when she was young and carefree.

She sighed and put her foot down on the gas pedal. Until Judd changed his mind about the Grattons, she would struggle to find the sunshine in her life.

The mortgage payment was due in three days. Madge needed her wages from George. She hated to ask, but she didn't have a choice. She brought it up when he came in for supper.

"I've been meaning to talk to you about that."

She heard the apology in his voice, and her lungs tightened.

"I'm afraid I can't pay you cash. By the time I paid the grocery bill and rent on this house, I had nothing left."

He'd tricked her. Led her to believe he'd pay her.

Was Judd right about this man? Was George nothing but a fake and a cheat?

"But I need the money."

He held up a hand in a conciliatory gesture. "I do have a suggestion. Mother has a car parked in Calgary. It's a fine vehicle. Much better than the one you drive. I propose I give it to you in lieu of wages. If you don't want it, you can sell it."

What good was a car? She needed money. Her chances of selling the vehicle were even more remote than his. Surely he knew it.

Sadly it seemed Judd was right. George used people to his own advantage.

"I'm sorry," George murmured. "I had expected to sell our belongings and have a little cash left over. It simply hasn't worked that way. I've made a mess of things for so many people. It seems I can add you to the list."

He sounded so contrite, she almost changed her mind. But no. He had cheated her.

Madge mumbled something completely unintelligible and staggered from the house. She climbed into her car and headed home. The mortgage payment was still due. She had to figure out a way to make up the deficit. If only she could talk this over with someone. But she didn't want to worry Mother. And Judd…well, Judd still hung about watching the house. He'd likely only point out that this confirmed his opinion of George.

She wished she could believe it didn't.

She pulled to the side of the road a short way from town and leaned over the steering wheel. *Lord God, why is this happening? Don't You care that we could lose our house?*

She recalled Grace's gentle voice. *All things work together for good.*

She didn't see how it was possible this time.

Lifting her head, she looked about and saw she had stopped within feet of the Cotton lane. Would Judd be there? She longed to be pulled into his arms and cradled against his chest, knowing her worries would diminish in his embrace.

Torn by her loyalty to and fondness of Grace, her disappointment and uncertainty about George and her hungry love for Judd, she couldn't think straight.

Before she could consider her actions or change her mind, she turned into the side road and drove toward the Cotton place.

Judd sat on the front step contemplating his choices—to continue with his quest to bring George to justice, and in so doing hurt another defenseless woman, or let it go, and in effect say what happened to his mother was of no consequence. Then there was the possibility that, unchecked, George would persist in his evil ways, and another innocent woman would end up hurt.

He buried his head in his hands. His plan had seemed simple and straightforward to start with. Now it had become tangled until he couldn't think straight.

At the sound of an approaching vehicle, he jerked to his feet. Someone might take objection to his trespassing. He jumped from the step and headed for the barn, where he might hope to remain hidden, though his car stood beside the shed and his belongings lay scattered about the kitchen.

He ducked out of sight before the vehicle reached the yard and pressed to the wall, straining to hear. The car drew to a halt. The motor died and quiet rang in his ears. Then footsteps sounded, and the door squeaked open. He held his breath, waiting for what would come next.

"Judd, are you here?"

Madge. His breath whooshed out at the sound of the familiar voice, and then his lungs refused to work. Madge. If he could just pull her into his arms and explain everything, he would feel a thousand times better.

He burst from the barn. "Madge, I'm here."

She raced straight toward him. He saw the eager longing on her face and broke into a jog, meeting her halfway across the yard. He opened his arms and she came into them, just like a horse headed for the open doors of a familiar barn. He pressed her close, her hot breath against his chest.

She shuddered.

"Madge, what's wrong?"

"Everything," she mumbled, clinging to him in a way that made him want to keep her forever close to his heart. "Nothing."

He chuckled. "'Nothing' doesn't make you shake like a leaf."

She lifted her head, her eyes hot with protest. "I'm not." But she shuddered again and laughed. "I am."

He pulled her close. Whatever had upset her, he would fix it. Slowly, so as not to make her leave his arms, he edged them toward the doorstep and sat down, turning her so she remained in his embrace. A grin caught his mouth and softened his eyes when she clung to him. "Now tell me what's wrong."

She rubbed her cheek against the fabric of his shirt, like Macat looking for attention.

He would gladly accommodate her need for comfort, and he stroked her hair.

She sighed. "Our mortgage payment is due tomorrow, and I don't have enough money. I'm not sure what to do."

"Is the banker apt to be lenient?"

"I expect he'll decide to foreclose."

Put them out of their home? Where would they

go? Judd had to fight to contain his anger at the injustice of the situation.

"I tried to get the banker to give us the house mortgage free when he sold the land, but he wouldn't."

Of course not. Bankers had to squeeze the last penny from defenseless widows and single young women. "How much do you still owe?"

"A lot." She named a sum that in better days would have been laughable but in the current situation was an impossible fortune.

"The house is worth much more than that, isn't it?"

"I expect the banker hopes so." She sighed against his chest.

He tightened his arm around her. He wanted to hold her safe and secure from every danger and threat. But he couldn't. Life contained too many unknowns, too many uncertainties. Slowly, words formed in his mind—a blend of what she'd said and what he'd learned in the past, though he hadn't been able to apply it to his life. He hoped she would find comfort in what he said. "I remember you telling me God was in control. He would do what was right and just."

She snorted. "How naive I was. Advice is easy for others. It's not so easy when I'm faced with an insurmountable barrier." She turned to look deep into his eyes. "I apologize for thinking I had solutions for your life because I clearly don't."

He couldn't bear the look of defeat in her gaze. "You didn't suggest you had the answers. You told me God did. That's a whole different thing."

She searched his eyes, looking past every defense he normally kept in place, delving into his secret hopes and dreams and, yes, beliefs. He hadn't applied the promise of God's care to his own situation, but he desperately wanted her to apply it to hers.

A slow, pleased smile caught the corners of her mouth and filled her eyes, and with a sigh of contentment, she again pressed her cheek close to his heart.

"Besides, what would the bank want with another house no one can afford to buy or even rent?"

A jolt shook her body. "Exactly."

They sat without speaking for a few minutes. He would have gladly stayed there until dark, holding her, feeling her trust. One thing nagged at his mind, though. "I thought you'd have money for this payment with the laundry you do and the work at Gratton's."

She seemed to hold her breath.

When she didn't answer, alarm snaked through his veins. "Did something happen?" He didn't trust George, but surely he wouldn't take advantage of Madge. If he had...Judd's fists curled. The size of his vengeance would not be measured.

She snorted. "Not like you're thinking. George is a good man. I'm a hundred percent convinced of it."

He lifted her from his chest to study her face. "Then why the doubtful tone?"

She wouldn't meet his gaze.

He caught her chin and for a moment considered kissing her rather than getting to the truth. He pushed the idea away—though not too far. He'd pursue that desire after he got the facts.

Slowly, reluctantly, she raised her eyelids and looked directly at him, regret filling her gaze. "He can't afford to pay me what he owes me."

He made an explosive sound. "The scoundrel."

She pressed warm fingers to his lips to quiet him. "Instead, he offered me a new car."

"Which won't pay the mortgage."

"No. It won't."

"I tried to warn you. That man must be stopped."

"Didn't you just assure me God is in control? Was it only idle words meant to soothe me?" She pushed from his arms. "Judd, I don't know what you believe. I don't think you do, either. I fear talk comes too easy for you." She stood, putting a cold six inches between them.

He reached for her, but she avoided his touch. He swallowed back an empty feeling that dried his insides as if they'd been blasted by the hot prairie wind. He didn't want to lose her. Not even for a moment or a few inches. "Madge, it isn't just words." But was it? Where did the words end and the believing begin? Did believing mean he walked away from George and what he did? "Don't I have a duty to stop George from doing further wrong?"

Her stubbornness faltered a moment. "Is it responsibility you seek, or is it a way to ease your guilt over not protecting your mother as you thought you should, whether or not she needed or wanted it? Seems to me if it's the former. You would be seeking the truth, not bullheadedly waiting for a way to exact your personal form of justice. There's a verse in the Bible that says, 'What doth the Lord require of thee, but to do justly and to love mercy and to walk humbly with thy God?'"

"Exactly. I'm seeking justice. That's what God requires of me."

"Only He asks us to combine it with mercy and humility. I think that would require you to investigate both sides of the picture."

He had all the facts he needed from his mother, though she'd been reluctant to admit them. Again, he reached for Madge, managed to catch her hand and draw her close. She let him pull her forward but stopped with a breath between them. She lowered her head so he saw nothing but the tangle of her dark curls. If that was all he could have, he meant to enjoy it and pressed his face into her hair, breathing in the sweetness of her.

He knew she wanted closeness as much as he did when she sighed. His insides flooded with love.

But then she slipped away and faced him.

"I am never certain who you are—Judd or Justin?"

He started to protest, but she held up her hand.

"And do you believe in trusting God? Or are you set on being in control?" She waited, but he had no answers.

Regret and resignation filled her eyes, and she nodded. "Until you know the answers to those questions, it is impossible for me to trust you." She turned on her heel and strode toward her car.

He reached for her but dropped his empty hand. She was right. Until he knew what he truly wanted and who he was, until he either took care of this business with George or…

He could think of no alterative and stood helpless as Madge drove away.

Madge's insides rolled and rebelled. She had gone for comfort and instead ended up more upset. Why was Judd so set on dealing with George? If he truly felt George was doing unethical things, then he should report him and let the law take care of it. But he seemed to want more than justice. Judd was discontent with how God handled things. It had come down to a trust issue. Could he trust God or not?

She sighed. And what about her? Did she believe God was to be trusted, no matter what? A few hours ago, she would have known the answer without hesitation. Of course she could trust God. So could Judd. Everyone could. But, with the threat of being evicted chomping at her heels, it was more difficult than Madge had ever suspected possible.

She managed to hide her worries from Mother and her sisters. That night she stood in her dark bedroom, staring out toward the Cotton place. From her window she saw the top of the barn. Nothing more. But she'd seen Judd's things in the house and imagined him there. She'd found comfort in his arms. Her heart longed to be with him, held close. She relived every word, every gesture of their embrace. But then reality had forced her to break away, had stolen the joy his arms had given.

Something he said triggered an idea: What did the bank want with another house they couldn't sell or rent?

She considered her options. It just might work.

Lord, I don't know what Mrs. Gratton's car is like. It may not serve the purpose at all. But—she fought a lingering, resistant moment of doubt—*I ask You to work things out. I trust Your love and care.*

Chapter Thirteen

Sally chatted next morning as they did laundry together. Madge appreciated her younger sister's help and conversation, but today her insides were too knotted with anticipation—or worry, if she were to admit it—to listen to Sally, and she let the words roll over her without any notice. Until a certain name entered the exchange.

"Are you still pining for Justin?" Sally demanded as they hung sheets.

"I'm not pining." Besides, Justin didn't even exist.

"I'm certain I saw him in town the other day. Is he still around?"

"I think he is." She was glad the sheets hid her face so Sally wouldn't see the heat rushing up her cheeks as she remembered how close he was and the precious few moments they'd shared. If only life didn't throw up such big roadblocks.

"Why doesn't he come calling? I thought he was a friend." Sally's voice gave a telltale quiver.

Madge sighed. Her little sister had always been too tender, too easily hurt. Madge vowed she'd do her best to avoid causing Sally pain. Losing the house would shake her to the core. Madge's heart turned to prayer. She needed God's divine intervention to carry out her plan.

She realized Sally waited for an answer to her question. "Justin is a friend, but perhaps right now he has other things to take care of." Until he did, he would be wise to stay away. Madge did not want her family in any way—even by association—involved with Judd's plans.

"I'm going to town early," she said after lunch. "George asked me to stop by today." Thankfully, neither Mother nor her sisters seemed to think it unusual. She turned to Sally. "Do you mind ironing the sheets for me?"

"Of course not. Macat and I will do it."

Madge's cat meowed from her perch in the window.

Content everyone would be happy in her absence, Madge drove from the yard. She automatically slowed as she passed the Cotton place. Every ounce of her heart cried out for her to stop and see if Judd was there. Perhaps try yet again to convince him to leave justice in God's hands. Not that she believed George needed justice.

If only there were some way she could mend the situation. But she couldn't without revealing Judd's secret—and she wouldn't go back on her word.

There was one thing she could do. Pray. It was enough. Her faith rested in God. She was about to challenge her trust and see if she could rely on it.

She chuckled at her convoluted reasoning. She was beginning to sound like Grace.

She slowed in front of the Gratton house but didn't stop. She intended to see George at the bank.

She went to the wicket and boldly informed Mr. August that she'd like to speak to Mr. Gratton.

George came out immediately. She followed him into a tiny office with a desk barely big enough for a sheet of paper and pen and ink.

"Madge, I want to say how sorry I am." He looked uncomfortable. "The banker informed me your mortgage payment is due tomorrow. I had no idea. I tried to persuade him to extend your credit…."

"Never mind that. I've reconsidered. I'll take the car in lieu of wages."

"I'll send for it tonight. Stop by tomorrow and you can take delivery of it. I vow I'll make it up to you at the first opportunity."

She left the bank without a backward look and

didn't draw a satisfying breath until she sat in her car. *Lord, please grant success to my plan.*

She moved woodenly through the next twenty-four hours, not daring to think what the future might hold, yet determined she would trust God as she faced it.

After lunch the next day, she drove to the Gratton house and went inside. Grace sat waiting for her. She held out a key.

"I think this is yours."

Madge faltered. "I understand it was your car. You don't mind giving it up?"

"Pshaw. George won't let me drive anymore, so what good is a car to me? He's afraid I might have one of my spells. Can you imagine? As if I would. They only come on when I'm overtired. Sometimes he treats me like a baby. I remind him I fed him bread and milk when he was small. Why, I could tell you things he did when he was a youngster that would make you see him in an entirely different light."

Madge held her palms toward Grace. "No, thanks." She had too many opposing views of the man already.

"I'm glad you're the one to get my car. Come on. I'll show it to you. It's out back."

Madge followed her. With a flair for drama, Grace

opened the door, bowed and waved her through. Madge gasped. "This isn't a car. It's a…it's a luxury."

"A DeSoto. Best of its class."

"It's wonderful." She raced down the steps to circle the car. "I heard about these but never expected to see one." A sleek beauty and much faster than her old Ford. The DeSoto had six cylinders, plus spoke wheels that gave it an extra classy feel, a split bumper and rumble seat. It would never be big enough for the family, but it would serve her purpose very well. In fact, it was beyond her dreams or expectations. *Thank You, God.* And to think she'd harbored doubts when she left the house this morning.

Grace handed her the key. "It's yours. Take it for a drive."

"I will." She climbed in, grinning so widely it hurt her face. She smoothed her hands over the soft seat and back and forth over the steering wheel. A lovely car. One to be proud of. She could almost imagine keeping it for herself. She sighed. That would defeat her purpose entirely, but before she went to the bank she'd take Joanie for a drive.

She parked in front of the Sharp home and sat behind the wheel, as proud as a princess at her coronation. The car handled like a charm, and the big motor purred with absolute confidence. Her grin did not flatten a bit as she went to the door and knocked.

Joanie answered and squealed. "It's about time you came to see me." She hugged Madge.

Madge knew the moment Joanie saw the automobile. Her squeal shifted to a sound of awe.

"Where did that car come from?"

"It's mine. Care to go for a drive?"

"Whoopie! In that thing? I guess I do." She called to tell her mother she was going out and raced toward the street. By the time Madge reached the driver's side, Joanie had squirmed into the new leather seat. "This is so nice." She shifted and faced Madge. "Spill it all. What did you do to get this fancy machine?"

"I worked for Mrs. Gratton. This will pay my wages, plus several more months of work." They drove through town, drawing more than one set of admiring eyes as Madge explained the deal. She hoped the banker would hear of the car in the next few minutes. "I'm not keeping it."

"Why not? It's beautiful."

"Not big enough for the family, though. And can you see me hauling laundry around in it?"

"A girl driving this kind of car shouldn't be doing laundry."

They both laughed at the way reality and fancy clashed in this automobile.

"How are Connie and his family doing?"

"Conrad," she corrected automatically. "They're

doing fine so far as I can tell, though to talk to Conrad you'd think it was all they can manage to get the little ones dressed every day."

"I suppose they're missing their mother."

"Of course. I didn't mean that. It's just, he refuses to see how I could help. He says it's too much to ask of me. Perhaps when the little girls are grown up, he says." She made a disgusted sound. "As if I intend to sit at home waiting ten or twelve years. No, siree. Not me."

"Maybe you'll find someone else." She knew Joanie would never entertain such an idea.

"Maybe I will."

"Joanie." Her voice revealed her shock. "I can't believe you said that."

Joanie sighed. "I guess I don't mean it, but I've got to do something."

It was such a familiar feeling. Seemed to have infected all those her age—her, Judd, Joanie—and she suspected others who had not said it aloud in her presence.

They left town, and Madge pulled to a stop at the side of the road so she could face Joanie and talk. She told of her worries about paying the mortgage and how she trusted God to take care of her in her need. "I believe this car is an answer I didn't imagine could be possible."

"This car? I don't understand."

"Banker Johnson won't be able to stand knowing someone else has the best car in town. I'm prepared to trade it for the mortgage. Though when I came up with the plan, I had no idea I would be getting such a nice car. I only knew I needed a bargaining chip in order to present any sort of option to the banker. I prayed God would make him willing to negotiate. But look. God has supplied far beyond what I could ask or imagine."

"Isn't that a Bible verse?"

"It is. My point is to ask God for an answer and trust Him to work it out."

Joanie looked doubtful. "I can trust God for me, but this is Conrad. He's so stubborn." She bounced around to stare out the front window. "It makes me want to march out there with the pastor and demand Conrad marry me on the spot."

Madge had a good laugh at the picture she imagined. Joanie, all fight and prickly, Connie, casting about for some place to hide and the preacher wondering what was going on. "You think it would work?"

Joanie's shoulders slumped. "Conrad would just get angry."

"Then you have no choice but to trust God to change Conrad's mind."

Joanie turned and studied Madge hard—hard enough to make Madge squirm. "I saw you with a man the other day. Who is this mysterious cowboy no one has ever seen?"

Madge struggled to hide her surprise. Judd seldom came to town as himself. "Where did you see us?"

"In Bowwell, at the play."

"You did? Why didn't you come over and say hello?"

Joanie laughed. "You seemed rather interested in the man. To the exclusion of glancing about with any concern at who else might be present." She giggled. "I could see stars in your eyes from across the room."

Madge groaned. She should have known someone would spot her. "You're sure you haven't seen the man before or since?"

"I think I would have noticed." The way she quirked her eyebrows and batted her eyes made Madge laugh.

"You have seen him. Promise you won't tell." Joanie nodded. Madge knew she could trust her friend without reservation. "He's Justin."

"Louisa's tutor? Oh, no. I would have recognized him."

"He's not teaching Louisa anymore. And it truly is him."

"You're sure?"

"Very sure."

"I get it. He really is the cowboy you plowed into.

But why was he hiding it? Where is he now? What is he doing?" Joanie almost burst with curiosity.

Madge picked one question to answer. "He has business to attend to."

Joanie studied her long and hard. "Aha. I see."

"What, pray tell, do you see?"

"You're in love with the man."

Madge snorted. "You just want everyone to be in love."

"Right. I want everyone to be as miserable as I am."

Madge would not confess she shared the emotion. Instead she started the car. "I have to get to the bank before it closes."

A few minutes later Madge drove to the front of the bank, feeling better than she had in some time. She paused behind the wheel to pray. *God, please let Mr. Johnson see this car and want it so bad he'll agree to my deal.* As she stepped to the sidewalk, she saw Mr. Johnson peeking out the window. She ducked her head to hide a grin. Seemed he'd heard about the car and had to see if the reports were true.

A few minutes later she left the bank with a valued piece of paper in her hands and the keys to the car in banker Johnson's. The man had been very eager to agree to her suggestion.

"Thank You, God," she murmured as she walked toward the Gratton place to retrieve the old, half-reliable car she was to own and repair for goodness knew how long into the future. She'd seen a few people reduced to pulling the motors out of their cars and hitching the chassis to a horse. They mockingly called them Bennett buggies after their Prime Minister, who seemed unable to do anything to stop the decline of the country. The Morgans could well come to the same situation. Only they didn't have a horse. But unable to find feed, farmers were abandoning them all over the country, letting them forage for themselves. Perhaps she would be able to get one really cheap, maybe even find a wandering one. She sighed. Then she would be faced with trying to find enough feed for a third animal. Her concerns were common; so many people suffered even worse fates as they had to sell their animals for mere pennies. Silently she beseeched God to end the drought.

As she neared the turnoff to the Cotton place, she slowed. Should she stop and tell Judd the success of her afternoon or leave him alone until he finished with this Gratton business? If only she could persuade him to let go of this ugly nonsense before he destroyed George and hurt Grace. Not physically, but emotionally. She had a responsibility to try again to get him to change his mind. She could speak from experience this time when she told him how God would take care of things.

She'd faced the same choice he must—trust God

or do it herself. God had answered beyond her expectations with the mortgage. She would trust Him to work in Judd's life, too.

God, keep him from hurting himself or another. Let him learn to depend on You to deal out justice.

For a moment she struggled with the desire to help God by speaking to Judd. She yearned to go to him and press her cheek against his chest, find sweet comfort and rest. She shook her head. Knowing he wanted to hurt, perhaps even destroy George, which would ultimately hurt Grace, made it impossible to give Judd her heart completely and wholly.

She continued homeward, propelled by the good news to share with her family.

Judd stared out across the dust-drifted yard. He ached all over, as if he'd shoveled a wagon full of grain in record time. However, the ache was not physical. It came from his heart. As if his blood had turned thick and struggled to flow through his veins. This strange malaise had started yesterday when he'd let Madge drive away. Not that he could have prevented her. She'd made that plain enough.

She'd wanted assurances he would let this go. Wanted him to leave this for God to handle. He had no doubt God would handle it. But that didn't prevent the man from doing more evil in the meantime. Nor did it give Judd a chance to get some sort of justice for his mother.

As the eldest, he should have been there to protect his mother. Instead, he'd been off pursuing his own adventures.

He jerked his head up. Madge had accused him of hunting George in order to ease his conscience.

No. It was more than that. Justice. Mercy. Humility. Madge had suggested he needed all three to justify his actions.

His insides rebelled at the idea. Justice he understood. The other two made him feel like a whiner. More fitting for Justin than Judd.

Takes a big man to admit he's wrong. Mother had said the words often as she tried to teach four boys to temper their adventures with gentleness. What would she think of his actions? He didn't have to think hard to know she'd side with Madge. He could see the pair of them standing shoulder to shoulder, their arms crossed over their chests, their eyes blazing.

"Good thing she isn't here." He had his hands full with Madge. He didn't relish the idea of a second fighter confronting him.

But right now he wished he had his arms full of Madge, her cheek pressed to his chest, her breath warm and sweet.

It was hard to contemplate mercy. He wasn't even

sure what it meant, except he was certain it required more than looking for retribution.

Humility was even harder. He had nothing to apologize for. But a huge dose of humility would be required to follow through on the idea just now forming in his mind with such stubbornness it could well be one of those settlers who dug in their heels and vowed they would not leave, come drought or high winds.

He didn't know if he could do it. Certainly went against his nature. But if the idea had come from God…

God, Madge is always talking about trust. I guess I need to trust You. I'm going to do this and see how things work out. It sounded like a qualified yes, and perhaps it was. But it was also a step of obedience.

He went inside and cleaned up. He studied himself in the mirror. Soon he'd shed the beard, but not now. He had something more important to take care of.

A glance at his clock revealed it was time. He crossed the yard to his car and drove to town, where he motored down the streets to the front of the Gratton house.

George would be home by now. Judd strode up the steps and knocked. When George opened the door, Judd said, "Can we talk? I have something you need to hear."

Chapter Fourteen

George's mother saw him. "Why, it's that nice Justin Bellamy I was telling you about. He came when Madge was here."

Judd stepped into the room. "Ma'am, I have a little confession to make. I'm really not Justin." He watched George. "My name is Judd Kirk."

George fell back a step. "Edna's son." His color faded like a white blind pulled over his face.

"That's right."

"What are you doing here? How is—" He swallowed hard. "How is your mother?"

"I guess as well as one could expect, considering." He would not speak of the matter in Grace's presence. "I'd prefer to talk to you in private."

George struggled to pull himself together, then nodded. "Come into the front room."

Grace sighed. "Obviously this business is much

too profound for a woman. I will wait in the kitchen." Sniffing, she marched regally into the far room.

Judd followed George and chose a straight-backed chair while George perched on the edge of the maroon sofa.

George cleared his throat. "What can I do for you?"

Judd thought he'd sorted it out, but now anger combined with pain at how much his mother had lost. "You stole my mother's savings and left her to face the consequences. She lost her house. While you—" He pointedly looked around the nice home the Grattons lived in. "You seem to have done well."

"I didn't steal her money. She gave it to me to invest. I promised she'd make a good return. But then the crash came and I lost it all."

How convenient to blame the crash. "Left her penniless." He curled his fists, warring a desire to plow them into the man's nose. "Never spoke to her after you did so."

"How could I face her?"

"Like a man."

"Her money is gone. My mother's money is gone. I foolishly thought I could make a fortune in the stock market. Instead, I lost it all. I ruined my mother as well as yours."

"How do you intend to repay it?" His voice was

brittle, unforgiving, but he would not accept any petty excuses.

"I can't." George's face wrinkled as if he fought back tears. "At least not now. But I will repay every penny if it takes the rest of my life."

"Noble words, but is she supposed to sit in abject poverty clinging to someday?"

George's face whitened even more, something Judd would have thought impossible. "Is she?"

"She lost every penny. What was she to do? It's only because she has three grown sons she isn't begging on the corner of a street, sleeping in alleyways." It was an exaggeration. Mother insisted she and Levi would manage quite fine. She would find work, maybe as a seamstress, and Levi was old enough to earn money, though they knew there were forty able-bodied men for every job. Nevertheless, she said they would be happy enough in a tiny house a friend had offered her.

George leaned over his knees, cradled his head in his hands. "I wanted to take care of her. We met at a church supper and became friends. I was so impressed with her. She had such eagerness for life. When she learned I worked in a bank and did investments, she asked me to invest her savings. She trusted me." He moaned. "I've ruined so many lives."

From this position, Judd saw a broken man. Pity stirred within his chest. Mercy? Was that what it was? Madge had suggested he seek the truth. He had to know. "What exactly did you do?"

George told a story of an opportunity presented to him by an acquaintance, a chance to double his money in a matter of weeks. "Fail proof," he said. "How could I be so gullible? So greedy?" Turned out the venture had disappeared into a bottomless pit like so many in the 1929 crash.

"Why didn't you tell my mother the truth?"

George closed his eyes and struggled for control. "You have to understand, I love her. But instead of caring for her, I ruined her. I couldn't face her."

Loved her? He hadn't considered that possibility and wasn't ready to accept it.

George gave Judd a demanding look. "Is she okay?"

"She's living with my brother."

"Please, don't tell her you've seen me. I want her to forget she's ever heard the name George Gratton."

"I can't give such a promise." He didn't know if he would have done his duty unless he informed his mother he'd seen George. Nor was he satisfied there was justice while George lived in this big house. He glanced about, noted with surprise the sparse furnishings.

George observed his interest. "This house is not mine. I'm here by the generosity of Mr. Johnson, who is related to my mother's cousin. We lost our house, most of our fine belongings, too. Everything except a few things Mother refused to part with. Like I said, I ruined my mother as well as yours. To my sorrow and shame."

He pushed to his feet and held out his hand. "You have my word that I will spend the rest of my life repaying my debt."

Judd refused the hand. "I've dealt with sneaky salesmen before. Words come easy, appear sincere, but beneath is a scheme. What's yours?"

George dropped his arm to his side and staggered back as if Judd had struck him. "I have no scheme. I have nothing but regrets."

"I've seen people coming and going late at night." Only one man, but maybe George would admit to more.

"There's been no one but Pastor Jones, who has come to offer me spiritual comfort."

Judd rose and stared out the window. It all sounded reasonable. But was it only smooth talk? How could he trust the man?

In his mind he pictured Madge, leaning forward, pleading as she told him to trust God to handle things. Was God asking the same thing? Yes, he knew he could trust God, but he was reluctant to trust men—one man in particular. But he was tired of sneaking around, pretending to be Justin Bellamy, forcing every thought to the task of watching George Gratton.

A smile pulled at his mouth. He might have tried to force every thought in that direction, but the vast majority of them headed down quite a different path to a pretty, intense, high-minded young woman and the way she fit so neatly in his arms and smelled of laundry soap and fresh air.

With a start he realized how foolish he looked, grinning as he stared out the window at nothing. He sobered and faced the man.

"I don't know if I buy your story or not. Be warned. I intend to remain in the area, and if you try cheating any other women out of their savings..."

George nodded. "You're welcome to keep an eye on me because I assure you I have nothing in mind but working hard so I can return your mother's money."

"Be that as it may." He headed for the door. As he reached for the handle, he paused. Seemed he was treating George in a way he wouldn't want his father treated if he were still alive. He slowly turned. "I hope you prove to be honest." He left without giving George time to reply. Far as he could tell, the man had said all he needed to. The proof lay in what he did from now on.

He drove to the store for a few supplies. The weekly paper, *Golden Prairie Plaindealer,* lay on the counter. He dropped his pennies on the dark wood and took a copy, then headed home.

The first thing he did was lather up his face and shave off the beard. No more Justin Bellamy. Then he sat down and read the news.

One item in particular caught his attention. He folded the paper to leave it on top, and he let himself dream and plan.

A knock sounded on the door as Madge and Sally cleaned the kitchen. Louisa and Mother had moved to the living room to write letters to the cousins and aunts back east.

Madge's heart clamored up her throat and clung there. Perhaps Judd had come calling.

"Who could that be?" Sally asked.

But Madge rushed to answer the knock, paused to calm her expression, then threw open the door. "Judd," she whispered. He was Judd. He wore the cowboy hat she remembered, his hair a dark fringe around the crown. He wore the shirt and pants she'd seen him in at their first encounter. And his beard was gone. She stared. Yes, strong chin and jawline, just as she remembered.

Sally had followed. "Justin? You look so different."

Judd jerked off his hat. "May I come in?"

Sally nudged Madge aside. "Don't worry about

her. She's just surprised to see you without your beard." She hissed at Madge, "Stop staring."

Madge jerked her gaze to the window but in truth saw nothing through it. She felt Judd in every pore. Breathed in a scent of shaving soap and prairie wool. What was he doing here? Why had he come as Judd?

"Sally, your sister seems to have forgotten her manners." Judd's voice rang with amusement.

Madge tried to pull herself together. It didn't do for him to see how much he surprised her. Practically tipped her off her feet, in fact.

"Invite me in. I'll explain everything to the whole family."

"Come along. Mother and Louisa are in the front room." Sally led the way.

Judd hesitated, waiting for Madge. She pulled herself together and followed Sally.

"This ought to be good," she whispered before they entered the room.

Louisa and Mother glanced up from their letter writing and gasped.

"Why, look at you," Mother said. "You look so strong and…"

"Tall," Madge said, suddenly enjoying the discomfort in Judd's face and the confusion in Louisa's.

"I have a confession to make."

"Not only is his beard gone, but his cough and limp are all better, too."

Judd sent a pleading look in her direction. "You aren't helping."

She giggled as joy began to paint her insides sunshine bright. Could this mean what she hoped it did? That he had settled his problems with George without wreaking havoc?

At his demanding nod, she sat down and folded her hands demurely.

"First, I must apologize for leading you to believe I was Justin Bellamy. My real name is—"

Madge couldn't stop staring at him and at the way he gave her quick, darting glances. She wondered if she made him nervous. The idea provided a great deal of pleasure.

He explained who he was and why he had felt he had to hide his true identity. "I confronted Mr. Gratton tonight."

Madge jerked forward so hard her neck protested. "You did?"

He nodded. "After much prayer, it seemed the right thing to do."

Their gazes locked as they exchanged silent messages of acknowledgement. He'd listened to her. Her heart could barely contain her joy.

Mother cleared her throat.

Madge slid her gaze away, knowing her cheeks were as red as they felt. Sally's giggle confirmed it.

"He said all the right things. How he hadn't meant

to lose Mother's money and was too ashamed to tell her face-to-face. He said he'd lost his mother's money, as well."

"Do you believe him?" Mother asked.

"I don't know. I'm not prepared to dismiss all my doubts."

Mother nodded. "Sometimes caution is wise."

"And what are your plans now, Justin?" Louisa giggled. "Whoops. I mean Judd."

"I'm not certain. I used to think I wanted to go back to being a cowboy, but it no longer feels right."

Mother smiled. "I'm sure you'll find what works for you." Her smile touched Judd, then angled toward Madge.

Madge lowered her eyes, lest Mother see how much she wanted to be part of his plans for the future.

"Can we offer you tea?" Mother asked, signaling to Sally to prepare it.

"Not today, though I'll gladly join you another time if I'm welcome."

"Of course you are. Anytime." Sally and Louisa murmured agreement.

Judd got to his feet. Madge stared at him. So tall. So handsome. All cowboy.

He faced Mother. "I'd like to take Madge for a drive, if that's okay with you."

"Why, it's just fine with me."

"Madge?" Judd reached for her hand.

She put her fingers in his firm palm and let him lead her from the room, wondering if her feet actually touched the floor.

He settled her in his car and drove from the yard.

"Where are we going?" She asked the question only in the hope he might believe she was thinking straight. In reality she didn't care where they went.

"To the Cotton place. There's something I want to show you."

"What?"

"You'll have to wait and see."

She turned to look out the side window, hiding her smile from him as memories of previous visits to the Cotton place danced through her mind. She had high hopes this visit would be even better.

A few moments later they stopped in front of the house. Judd raced around and opened the door for her, took her hand, pulled it around his elbow and pressed it to his forearm.

A thrill of expectation rippled through Madge. She longed to turn immediately into his embrace, but Judd had something else in mind and led her toward the house. "I'm so pleased to hear you resolved things with George."

Judd squeezed her fingers. "At first I only wanted to please you so you would spend time with me. But then I really felt I had to trust God. I intend to keep an eye on George." He chuckled. "It's not like God needs my help. Maybe I'm still learning exactly what trust means."

"Oh. I haven't told you how God answered my prayer." They reached the house, but rather than go inside, they sat on the step, much as they had done not very long ago. She gladly snuggled close to his chest, reveling in his nearness. "Something you said gave me an idea."

"I don't recall saying anything profound."

"I guess it just comes naturally for you." She giggled and nuzzled her cheek against his shoulder.

He squeezed her tight. "Maybe you are too easily impressed. Exactly what did I say?"

"You asked what the banker would want with another house he couldn't sell or rent."

"I did? Must have slipped out unnoticed. If I remember correctly, I was somewhat distracted by a certain pretty miss."

She sat up, breaking from his arms, and pretended shock and hurt. "You've been seeing someone else?"

He blinked, startled by her question, then he grabbed her in mock fierceness. "I have eyes for no one but you." He sobered as he looked deep into her soul.

She grew still. Searched his gaze, and found love and belonging in his heart. With a sigh that came from the depths of her being, she leaned toward him.

His eyes darkened to midnight, and he caught her mouth in a gentle kiss.

Several intense heartbeats later she snuggled against his chest. "I was about to tell you how God answered my problem before you interrupted me."

His chuckle rumbled below her ear. "Some delays are worth it."

"Umm." For a moment she didn't speak, so content she was loath to move.

"About the mortgage?" he prompted.

"Oh. Yes." She sat up and faced him so she could keep her thoughts in order, though at the look in his eyes and the way his gaze kept dropping to her mouth, her mind seemed full of peanut butter.

"The mortgage?"

"I told you George had offered me a car in exchange for the work I did. Even though I had no idea what sort of car it would be, I hoped it would prove a bargaining chip with the banker. I wanted to offer him a trade for two or three months' payments."

Judd nodded. "Good idea."

"You should have seen the car." She laughed, then described it. "Banker Johnson saw me drive up and was already drooling by the time I got to his office. I explained I didn't have enough money for the whole payment. He kept looking outside to the car. When I casually suggested I might be able to trade something, he almost jumped from his chair." She savored the feeling of victory for another moment. "In the end I walked out with the mortgage in my hand—free and clear—and he got the car he drooled over." She shivered playfully. "Isn't that great news?"

He pulled her to his chest and held her so close they breathed as one. "It's the best news."

She wondered at the way his voice caught, then forgot everything but the sweetness of his embrace.

With a deep sigh he eased her back. "Come inside. I want to show you something." He pulled her to her feet and kept his arm about her as they went into the kitchen.

He'd tidied since she'd been here last. Dust no longer layered every surface. The table gleamed, and the floor—she gasped. "It's clean enough to eat on."

"I pulled up the old linoleum and found a very nice wooden floor beneath. You like it?"

"It's beautiful. But why are you going to all this work on someone else's house?"

He led her to the table and held a chair for her. She sat, though she wondered at his delay. What did he have to show her that required she sit? Tension trickled across her shoulders.

"Look at the paper."

She pulled the newspaper toward her. A page of notices and advertisements. Nothing to hint at the cause of Judd's barely concealed excitement. "Exactly what am I supposed to notice?"

He tapped one ad. "Read it."

She read aloud: "'Property to be sold for back taxes. Farm with house and barn. Excellent property. Taxes to be paid by cash or service to the municipality. For more information or to take possession please contact…'" She glanced at Judd. "I don't understand. Notices like this appear all the time."

"Not like this. Finish reading the ad."

"'Property formerly owned by Jacob Cotton.' It's this place."

"Yes. I'm getting it." He pulled her to her feet. They stood in each other's arms, yet with inches between them. He searched her face as if desperate for her reaction.

"You'll be living here? So close?" Her joy began as a tiny bud and blossomed to a full-blown wildflower. She knew her feeling was evident in her eyes. She didn't know how to keep it under control and buried her face into his shirtfront to hide it.

His arms tightened around her. "I hoped you'd like the idea."

She did. Oh, how she did. To have him so close she had only to run across the fields to visit him. He could do the same to see her. They'd be able to attend church together, go on outings.

He eased back to look in her face. "Madge, I love you. I want to marry you and share my life and this place with you."

Her joy caught in her throat. Tears stung her eyes.

Judd's expression grew uncertain. "Surely you guessed how I feel. Shoot. I should have waited."

She found her voice. "No need to wait. I love you, too."

"You'll marry me?"

Reality hit with the suddenness of a clap of thunder, shuddering through her. She pressed her lips tight to stifle a cry. Sniffing back tears, she shook her head. "Judd, how can I? Who will take care of my family?" And what about Louisa? Yet it hurt like mad to refuse him.

His smile turned to stone. "You said the mortgage was paid."

"But we still have to eat. Pay for gasoline. They count on me to earn the cash." And what about Louisa? The question again thundered through her head.

He dropped his arms and stepped away.

"Judd." Her voice protested even as her heart ripped like torn paper. "We'll be close."

He strode to the window and stared out, his shoulders heaving as if he'd run ten miles.

Madge pressed her knuckles to her mouth. Had she lost him? Agony like a deep cut filled her. *Lord, help him understand.*

Slowly he turned. She expected anger, hurt, disappointment. Instead he smiled—a look of such patience and hope she couldn't believe her eyes.

He crossed the room and held out his arms.

Without hesitation she let him pull her to his chest. She shuddered as she thought how close she'd come to losing him.

"I'm sorry. I shouldn't have reacted like that."

She clung to him. How she longed to be able to find such comfort any time she wanted it. But she couldn't abandon her family. She must explain the turn of affairs to Louisa before she could accept his offer of marriage.

Judd shifted so her cheek lay in the hollow of his shoulder. "I think we've both forgotten a very important fact—God is in control. He will provide an answer. It surprises me we should forget when we've both experienced His help in just the past few hours. Madge, my sweetheart, I am going to pray and trust God to give us a solution because—" He turned her to search her face.

She thrilled at the warmth of his love, clearly visible in every line and feature.

"Because I don't want to waste one moment of being together and loving you."

Hope and trust grew as she met his look. "I, too, will pray."

"God will provide a way."

She nodded. Judd's complete assurance left no room for a shadow of doubt.

He kissed her again and then took her through the house, showing her the things he had done. Besides dusting and cleaning and removing curled and cracked linoleum, he had repaired broken window frames and rehung a sagging screen door.

"Everything looks so good." She longed for the day she could share it with him as his wife. Although she couldn't imagine how it would be possible with her family needing her, but she would do as Judd advised—trust God.

How sweet to have him tell her those words. Almost as sweet as hearing, "I love you."

One day soon—God willing—she'd hear them every morning when she wakened.

Chapter Fifteen

Five days had passed since Judd's proposal. He'd attended church with them as Judd Kirk. His presence was sweet torture for Madge, as nothing changed to make her feel she could accept his offer of marriage. And how she longed to. Every thought, every breath ached for it. Even as she hung sheets, she thought of the joy she would get hanging sheets of her own.

Judd reminded her to trust and pray. How she laughed at his urging. "Ironic how my words are being quoted back to me."

He grinned. "Just proves how well I listen. I'll make you a very good husband. Always ready to heed your advice."

"If it suits you." She struggled to keep her voice teasing when she really wanted to wail against the need to wait.

Monday morning arrived and with it, laundry to

do. Not needing to make a mortgage payment, she'd cut down on her customers. She still owed George and Grace for the car, and for that she worked two afternoons a week. Even with reduced customers she kept busy. Of course, she stole as much time from her work as possible to run over to the Cotton place.

Sally put some wet sheets through the wringer. "When are you and Judd getting married?"

Thankfully she bent over the washtub so she could keep her face hidden from Sally. Surely if her sister saw her, she would see the longing. Forcing false cheerfulness into her voice, she answered, "I don't have time."

Sally grew still. "I never thought marriage to be considered an obligation you had to schedule in."

Madge hoped her sister would drop the conversation.

Instead Sally shifted to study Madge more closely. Madge kept her head over the tub, even though she had no more need to. Finally she couldn't bend anymore without ending up sore, and she straightened and made a show of arching her back, pressing her hands to her hips.

Still Sally waited.

"What?" Madge asked.

"Will you ever see me as anything but your little sister, too young to be counted an equal?"

The question caught Madge by surprise, and she stared at Sally. "What are you talking about?"

"You know. And you don't fool me. You think you have to keep doing this job." She pointed toward the washtubs. "Even though you found a way to pay off the mortgage, you can't stop being in charge. You can't believe I could do this job. You—you—"

Madge gaped. She'd never seen her sister so upset.

Sally planted her hands on her hips and drew in a deep breath. "You think you have to stay here and look after us. As if you can take Father's place. As if—" Sally began to build up steam again. "As if I couldn't do my share. Fine." She spun on her heel. "Forget marriage with a fine man like Judd, and stay home and be a martyr if that's what you want." She stomped toward the house and slammed the door after her.

"Sally?" Her little sister had a temper? Who would have guessed it? She turned back to the laundry, then paused and stared at the wringer. Sally thought she could manage? Could she? She'd accused Madge of trying to replace Father. She wanted to deny it, but a sliver of truth caught at her protests and dug in with a vengeance.

She thought of the decision to sell the land and keep the house, the arrangement for a lowered mortgage, even the deal to trade the car for the mortgage. Then there was the sale of the horses and all but a milk cow. Everything had been at her suggestion, with Mother's approval. Madge groaned. She *was* guilty of thinking she had taken Father's place. It gave her a sense of control, as if she could single-handedly keep the depression away from their door. And, too, it made Father feel close. Perhaps she strove for his approval even though he was gone.

Judd had urged her to pray and trust God. She had prayed and thought she trusted. But in this area she felt she must work. She hadn't even considered the family might not need her as much as she thought they did. But even if they could manage without her, there remained the problem of Louisa. How could she face her sister knowing she had taken Judd away?

God, show me the answer in this.

First, she must speak to Mother. She found her in the front room darning stockings. "Mother, Judd has asked me to marry him."

Mother smiled. "I know. He told me."

"You aren't upset that I…" She struggled for a word that didn't make her feel guilty, then gave up. "I stole him from Louisa?"

"You can't steal something that doesn't belong to another person. He never saw her the same way he sees you."

"But Louisa—"

Louisa burst into the room. "I saw how it was between you two. Yes, at first I thought he belonged to me." She colored prettily. "At first he seemed ideal, but then he began to talk of adventure, ranching in the west and all sorts of things I wouldn't have enjoyed. And his eyes blazed whenever Madge entered the room. It was making me miserable to try and keep his attention on me. So…" She ducked her head and spoke very quietly. "I decided to play matchmaker instead."

Madge laughed. "So that's why you sent us to the play."

"You enjoyed it, didn't you?"

"I did." She smiled, her heart full of sweet memories. "You're sure you're not angry?"

"I'm happy for you." She opened her arms, and the girls hugged.

Madge turned back to Mother. "I haven't said yes because I wasn't sure you could manage without me."

Mother rolled away the yarn and stuck the large needle in the ball, then pulled Madge to her side. "Madge, you have been a real help. We couldn't have managed without you. I'm proud of how hard you've worked, and your father would be, too."

Madge nodded and blinked back tears. She needed to hear those words.

"Thanks to you, our home is now secure. And it's time for you to move on with your own life. I had hoped Justin would be suitable as Louisa's husband, but I'm nothing but happy he is suitable as yours. We will be fine without you." She patted Madge's hands. "And you and Judd will be close if we need help."

Peace flowed through Madge.

"What are you waiting for?" Mother asked. "Go to him."

With a burst of happy laughter, Madge sprang to her feet. "I will. I am." She hugged Louisa again, then rushed outside where Sally had returned to the laundry and skidded to halt. She should stay and help. But really, did she need to? "Sally, can you finish here? I want to see someone."

Sally turned, saw the look on Madge's face and laughed. "I can do this with one hand tied behind my back. Now get out of here. Leave me alone." She turned back to the task. "And give Judd a kiss for me."

Sally's laughter followed Madge as she raced across the field. She was out of breath by the time she reached the Cotton place. "Judd?" she yelled.

He bolted from the barn, took one look at her and dropped his hammer to sprint to her. He studied her face.

"I've come to say yes." She smiled welcomingly, then laughed as he swept her off her feet and twirled her around.

Epilogue

Three months later

Madge looked at herself in the mirror in the side room of the church. The pale blue dress Sally had made her emphasized the sparkle in her eyes. Louisa had done her hair, pulling it into an upsweep, then allowing the unruly curls to fall around Madge's face.

Sally's likeness appeared beside Madge's. "You glow." She hugged Madge. "I'm so happy for you."

Louisa's face appeared over her other shoulder. "You deserve every bit of happiness. I pray for nothing but the best for you and Judd."

Madge shifted to meet Louisa's eyes. "You don't hold any resentment that I stole him from you?"

Louisa giggled. "You can't steal something I never owned. He never saw anyone but you. I'll trust God to bring me a man who looks at me the way Judd looks at you."

Mother poked her head through the door. "Girls, it's time."

The three of them peered into the mirror a moment longer, smiling.

"Come on," Louisa urged.

"Yeah, you've kept him waiting long enough," Sally said. "Insisting you had to work at Gratton's."

"I had to pay off the car."

"We know," the girls chorused.

Sally went down the aisle first, then Louisa. Madge followed. She'd promised herself she'd concentrate on everything so the details would be forever branded in her memory, but as soon as she saw Judd, she forgot all else. He wore a black suit and white shirt, but despite them he had a rugged outdoor look. He loved working outside and had managed to locate enough feed for a few head of cows.

"The drought will end, and when it does I'm going to be ready with a herd while others are scrambling to find replacement cows," he'd told her one night as they discussed their future.

Together they had cleaned and polished the house and collected odds and ends of furniture to add to the things left behind by the Cottons.

At the front pew, Mother held out her hand and Madge paused to squeeze it. She turned to take

Judd's mother's hand and smiled past the woman, at George.

Mrs. Kirk had come to help with preparations and meet Judd's intended. She'd seen George downtown and broken into tears.

Judd had grown angry. "That man should have left town."

"I'm very glad he didn't," Mrs. Kirk had said, then had dried her eyes and crossed the street to speak to him.

"Seems your mother is ready to forgive him," Madge had murmured.

"She's just asking for more trouble."

But Mrs. Kirk had told Judd she'd had nothing to forgive. "He made a mistake and he feels bad about it. I don't intend to let it form a barrier. Life is too short for pettiness."

Judd had sputtered and protested, but his mother did not relent. Eventually Judd had admitted his mother seemed happy.

"Shouldn't that be what matters?" Madge had asked.

Judd had swept her into his arms and kissed her soundly. "How can I protest when I'm so content with life? I can only hope she is so happy."

Now Madge turned from those in the pews to face Judd, and her heart swelled against her ribs in supreme joy.

"I love you," she mouthed.

"I love you," he mouthed back.

People chuckled. Apparently anyone watching could also read his lips.

She didn't care. She didn't care if the whole world knew of their love.

Judd reached for her, drew her to his side and kept her there until the preacher announced they were man and wife. Then he turned and kissed her before God and these witnesses.

"God is good," she murmured against his lips.

"And we'll prove it over and over in the years to come."

They turned to receive congratulations and good wishes from their friends and neighbors.

Life, Madge knew, would be sweet and precious shared with this wonderful man.

* * * * *

Dear Reader,

My grandparents lived through the Great Depression—and so much more. My grandmother, especially, never got over the fear of being without basic necessities. She was determined to never again be caught without things we take for granted. This led her to keep stuff others could see no use for, like bits of string rolled into a large ball, every newspaper and magazine that came into the house and pencil stubs so short it was impossible to hold them (she put them in a pen cap to give them a little added length). I think a person would have to endure what she did in order to understand her reasons for holding on to simple, ordinary things.

In my story, Madge is equally determined to save her family from so many things. I found it interesting to wonder how my faith would stand up to the challenges my characters faced.

I hope I was able to portray their struggles in a realistic way, yet one that portrays hope and trust in God's unfailing care.

God bless,

Linda Ford

Questions for Discussion

1. The Depression is upon the Morgan family. Is this the only factor influencing Madge's view of life? Are there other factors? Are they past, present or future? Is she aware of them?

2. How have these factors impacted Madge's way of dealing with things?

3. Is she right or wrong in her beliefs? What would you say to her regarding her life if you met her?

4. Judd is driven by a specific event. What is it? Is there more to it than what he says?

5. Is he seeking justice, revenge or something else entirely?

6. Madge and Judd's first meeting is quite different from their second. How would the romance have differed if the second meeting had been their first? Or would it have been different?

7. Do you think Judd was justified in hiding his true identity? Why or why not? What alternative action would you suggest for him?

8. Madge believes God will see her through every crisis in her life. Are there times you see this at work? Times you wanted to remind her of her faith?

9. Mrs. Morgan is determined to find a husband for Louisa. How do you think she felt when Judd and Madge fell in love? What do you think Mrs. Morgan will do next?

10. These characters lived during the Great Depression. Times were tough. What challenges did they face that were specific to their era? Do we face similar challenges today?

11. What did Judd have to learn in order to be ready for love?

12. What did Madge have to learn in order to be ready?

13. What challenges do you foresee for them in the future? How do you think they will handle them?

INSPIRATIONAL

Wholesome romances that touch the heart and soul.

Love Inspired

celebrating 15 YEARS

HISTORICAL

COMING NEXT MONTH
AVAILABLE FEBRUARY 14, 2012

THE COWBOY FATHER
Three Brides for Three Cowboys
Linda Ford

HOMETOWN CINDERELLA
Ruth Axtell Morren

THE ROGUE'S REFORM
The Everard Legacy
Regina Scott

CAPTAIN OF HER HEART
Lily George

Look for these and other Love Inspired books wherever books are sold, including most bookstores, supermarkets, discount stores and drugstores.

LIHCNM0112

REQUEST YOUR FREE BOOKS!

2 FREE INSPIRATIONAL NOVELS
PLUS 2
FREE
MYSTERY GIFTS

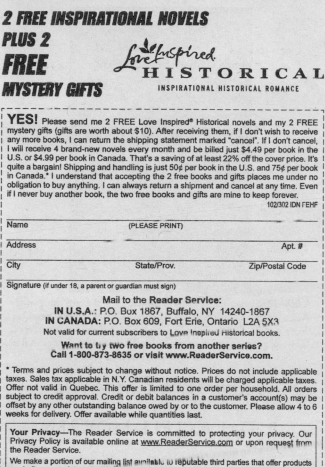

Love Inspired.
HISTORICAL
INSPIRATIONAL HISTORICAL ROMANCE

YES! Please send me 2 FREE Love Inspired® Historical novels and my 2 FREE mystery gifts (gifts are worth about $10). After receiving them, if I don't wish to receive any more books, I can return the shipping statement marked "cancel". If I don't cancel, I will receive 4 brand-new novels every month and be billed just $4.49 per book in the U.S. or $4.99 per book in Canada. That's a saving of at least 22% off the cover price. It's quite a bargain! Shipping and handling is just 50¢ per book in the U.S. and 75¢ per book in Canada.* I understand that accepting the 2 free books and gifts places me under no obligation to buy anything. I can always return a shipment and cancel at any time. Even if I never buy another book, the two free books and gifts are mine to keep forever.

102/302 IDN FEHF

Name	(PLEASE PRINT)
Address	Apt. #
City	State/Prov.	Zip/Postal Code

Signature (if under 18, a parent or guardian must sign)

Mail to the Reader Service:
IN U.S.A.: P.O. Box 1867, Buffalo, NY 14240-1867
IN CANADA: P.O. Box 609, Fort Erie, Ontario L2A 5X3

Not valid for current subscribers to Love Inspired Historical books.

Want to try two free books from another series?
Call 1-800-873-8635 or visit www.ReaderService.com.

* Terms and prices subject to change without notice. Prices do not include applicable taxes. Sales tax applicable in N.Y. Canadian residents will be charged applicable taxes. Offer not valid in Quebec. This offer is limited to one order per household. All orders subject to credit approval. Credit or debit balances in a customer's account(s) may be offset by any other outstanding balance owed by or to the customer. Please allow 4 to 6 weeks for delivery. Offer available while quantities last.

Your Privacy—The Reader Service is committed to protecting your privacy. Our Privacy Policy is available online at www.ReaderService.com or upon request from the Reader Service.

We make a portion of our mailing list available to reputable third parties that offer products we believe may interest you. If you prefer that we not exchange your name with third parties, or if you wish to clarify or modify your communication preferences, please visit us at www.ReaderService.com/consumerchoice or write to us at Reader Service Preference Service, P.O. Box 9062, Buffalo, NY 14269. Include your complete name and address.

LIH11B

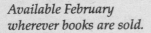